ELIZA PROKOPOVITS

Her Fae Secret

Special Annotated Edition

Copyright © 2025 by Eliza Prokopovits

All rights reserved. No part of this publication may be reproduced, stored or transmitted in any form or by any means, electronic, mechanical, photocopying, recording, scanning, or otherwise without written permission from the publisher. It is illegal to copy this book, post it to a website, or distribute it by any other means without permission.

First edition

*This book was professionally typeset on Reedsy.
Find out more at reedsy.com*

To Patricia C. Wrede, whose books showed me that Regency London can be full of magic.

Contents

Foreword	ii
Acknowledgments	iv
Chapter 1	1
Chapter 2	22
Chapter 3	35
Chapter 4	46
Chapter 5	58
Chapter 6	67
Chapter 7	79
Chapter 8	91
Chapter 9	99
Chapter 10	111
Chapter 11	121
Chapter 12	133
Chapter 13	143
Chapter 14	149
Chapter 15	158
Chapter 16	169
Chapter 17	181
Chapter 18	189
Chapter 19	199
Chapter 20	209
Epilogue	217
Also by Eliza Prokopovits	224

Foreword

Please note: This is a special **annotated** edition, which means you'll be seeing occasional notes from me throughout the book with thoughts on the characters, inspiration, etc. You'll also get lots of underlined sections.

As this is a special edition, and as the point is to share a glimpse into the writing of the book, I want to start with a note about *Her Fae Secret*'s inspiration on the whole.

It began, as so many things do for me, with reading. Patricia C. Wrede has several lovely books set in a magical Regency London—I've read *Sorcery and Cecelia* multiple times, and I had just reread it and her duology of *Mairelon the Magician* and *Magician's Ward*. I was, as always, enamored with both the Regency setting and the magic, and I wondered if I could create my own magical Regency England. (That is actually a very common starting point for me: "I wonder if I could…" And it turns out, I frequently can.) And then I wondered if I could retell fairy tales there, because why *wouldn't* you want to include fairy tales? So I began wondering what fairy tale would be best suited to the balls and elegance of Regency London.

As you can guess, I settled on The Twelve Dancing Princesses, since dancing and balls are quite literally the core of the story.

I gave them a new reason to go into Faerie, as I've never much liked the versions in which they're cursed—I love dancing, and other than the sheer exhaustion of dancing all night every night, it actually sounds like more fun than curse to me. I also cut the number of princesses from twelve to three, because twelve is a lot and I do better with small casts, but I still wanted to keep the sister dynamics.

When I started writing, I intended *Her Fae Secret* to be a standalone story, just a fun experiment to see if it was possible. And, truthfully, when it was done, I moved on to a different experiment—seeing if I could blend a cozy mystery with a fairy tale (*The Thunderstone Theft*, which I published first but wrote second). But then I couldn't stop thinking about what other fairy tales could end up blended with Regency magic, with Beauty and the Beast, my long-time favorite, claiming the next experimental spot. Within the first two pages, writing *The Beast's Magician* felt like coming home, and so the series grew.

Enjoy!
-Eliza

Acknowledgments

Thanks to everyone who believes in me and encourages me. To God, who gives me inspiration, hope, and all that I need; to my wonderful husband and unwaveringly supportive friends; to my parents and my kids; to my editor, Megan Records, and my cover designer, Karri Klawiter; to you, my readers: thank you.

Chapter 1

Eleanor sat by the window with her spell book laid out on the table. She pulled it closer to make out a difficult word. She'd written her own notes all over this page, and sometimes her tiny script obscured the original. She sighed and sat back, closing the book. *Ford's Magical Accomplishments for Young Ladies*. The title was faded, and the leather of the cover was scuffed and worn. This copy had been Mama's when she was young. Indeed, some of the notes in the margins were in Mama's flowing handwriting. Mama had insisted that they practice all the usual accomplishments—singing, dancing, drawing, playing the pianoforte, and magic—but with an emphasis on magic. Eleanor didn't mind at all; magic was her favorite. She knew nearly all of Ford's book by heart, including the extra notes.

Ford's Magical Accomplishments for Young Ladies is inspired by Fordyce's Sermons to Young Women, which Mr. Collins reads aloud in Pride and Prejudice. (He approves; the young women in question do not.)

"Eleanor, dear, what new accomplishment are you practicing? You've been squinting again."

Eleanor blinked up at her aunt. "I'm sorry, Aunt. Some of the spells are hard to make out."

"Was your squinting worthwhile?"

Eleanor smiled. She reached over to the candelabra on the table and touched the wick of each candle, concentrating on the spell-word as she did. They flamed to life, one after another.

Sophie applauded.

"I'm hoping to learn to light them without touching them," Eleanor sighed.

"You will," Anne said. "But that was well done—you haven't needed to whisper the words in ages."

Silence was a sign of skill, Mama had told them. It was accepted that young ladies would speak their spells, as part of the performance, but magicians trained at Oxford or Cambridge were expected not to. It was one of the many double standards within English magic. Illusions and small parlor tricks were the purview of high-born young ladies; discussions of magical theory and executing spells of power were restricted to university-educated men. And for the poor, access to spells or magical training was near nonexistent.

The unfairness of it rankled Eleanor. But she made the most of her training, and like Mama, she never spoke her spells.

CHAPTER 1

This is not my only book in which women go against common magical practice and double standards. Isabelle in *The Beast's Magician* also challenges the prevailing mindset, and Bianca in *Her Cursed Apple* simply learns every spell she can get her hands on and flaunts the system.

"I hadn't noticed how dark it was getting until you lit the candles," Aunt Everley said. "Ring for tea, Anne, and then we must dress. Thank goodness your new gowns arrived from the modiste today."

"I still fail to see why a lack of new dresses ought to keep us from entering London society at Lady Sterling's ball," Eleanor said. "The gowns we brought with us from home are perfectly elegant."

"Oh, Eleanor, we've been over this," Aunt Everley said. "You're being presented to the *ton*. You need to look your best. First impressions are everything."

Sophie wrinkled her nose. "I agree with Eleanor. I just want to go to the ball and dance." She executed a little twirl in the center of the room, her light brown hair coming half loose from its pins and wisping around her face.

Sophie's a bit like Kitty and Lydia from *Pride and*

Prejudice, where the only thing they need to enjoy a ball is to never be without a dance partner.

"Yes, well, you're young enough that dancing is all you need to care about." Anne went to the table to clear space for the tea tray that she accepted from the maid who appeared promptly at the parlor door. "You could have a second, or even a third, Season if you wanted to."

"And *whose* choice was it to wait until you were one-and-twenty?" Aunt Everley said pointedly.

Anne pursed her lips.

Eleanor spoke up. "We all agreed together to come out at the same time. One-and-twenty isn't so very old."

"It is for a debut Season," Aunt Everley said firmly. "Even Sophie could have come out two years ago."

"Eighteen is plenty young enough to be finding a husband," Eleanor protested. "Besides, now that peace has finally come, all the officers are home, with money and time and no one to share them with."

Which places this book in about 1815, after the Battle of Waterloo. Napoleon has been banished to St. Helena.

Sophie laughed. "And some of them with titles to inherit."

CHAPTER 1

"But I wish, Anne, that you wouldn't get so worried about making a good match. I'm sure it will all work out." Eleanor stepped over and planted a kiss on the top of her elder sister's dark blonde head.

"It's not just about making a match," Anne murmured, pouring tea. "If all I wanted was a husband, Aunt Everley and Papa could have one arranged before the Season's half over. I want—"

"Passion and romance," Sophie declared dreamily, plopping into her seat.

"Don't interrupt," Anne chided, smiling as she handed Sophie a cup. "I'd be happy with friendship and compatibility. Passion may not last, but friendship would set us up well for life."

Maybe unsurprisingly, Anne is inspired by Jane Bennet, the oldest sister in *Pride and Prejudice*.

Sophie made a face. "I won't settle for less than being swept off my feet."

Aunt Everley tutted. "Love matches are all well and good, but it's possible to have a happy marriage even when it's arranged for other reasons. Your uncle and I did just fine together."

Eleanor spoke up to prevent Sophie from arguing with their aunt. "I want what Mama and Papa had," she said softly. "I want respect and admiration."

"And adoration." Anne smiled. "They worshipped each

other."

Aunt Everley's expression softened. "They did. Your mother made your father a better man, and he was a good one to begin with." She looked at the three of them and heaved a sigh. "Well, I hope you all find what you're looking for, but I also hope you'll keep your heads about you."

"We will," the girls assured her together.

"None of us are in a rush," Eleanor added.

"Except Anne," muttered Sophie.

"Well, I'm three years older than you."

"You're the best of us at conversing with strangers, and you're lovely," Eleanor said, half teasing. "The *ton* will be so enamored by you that they won't even notice Sophie or me."

"Sophie has the best figure." Anne waved off the teasing. "And you, Eleanor, look like a Greek goddess just stepped off your pedestal in that new white silk."

"I always saw us as three Muses," Sophie said. "Alike, but different. If one of us does well, I'm sure the others will too."

Eleanor grinned at her younger sister's romantic view. At age nine, Sophie had sweet-talked their father into teaching her to read Greek. Since then she'd spent all her free hours reading Greek poetry in the shade by the stream, or else dancing through wildflower meadows in bare feet. Perhaps Anne wasn't entirely wrong in suggesting that Sophie could do with an extra Season or two before settling down to running her own home.

Anything Greek was very popular at the time. The Elgin

CHAPTER 1

Marbles (pieces of the Parthenon maybe-not-so-ethically obtained) had been put on display in London, and the obsession with ancient Greece could be seen in popular dress styles.

Eleanor took a sip of her tea, but her stomach was a nervous tangle over their evening plans. *You're being ridiculous*, she told herself. *It's just another ball.* Balls were nothing new; Father hosted at least one every summer at Fairfield Hall, and all three girls were excellent dancers. But this was the *beau monde*, and every single person there would be assessing the new arrivals, judging their worth as friends, rivals, or potential matches.

"When we saw Lady York at the milliner's the other day, what was she saying, aunt?" Anne asked. "Something about Almack's?"

"She suggested that Almack's was the best place for you to appear first," Aunt Everley said dismissively. "There are merits—whoever the patronesses approve are set up well for the Season—but Almack's is rather intimidating for a first foray into Society. Lady Sterling's ball will be more prestigious and more elegant, and I dare say Lady Cowper and Lady Castelreagh will be there anyway. They are all quite good friends."

"And we've met Lady Sterling," Sophie said. "She's not as terrifying as I expected a countess to be."

Eleanor grinned. "That's probably because she likes Aunt Everley."

"She likes you girls too," Aunt Everley said. "In all, she's an excellent person to know on your introduction to Society."

When they'd finished tea, they retired upstairs to dress for the ball. Eleanor shrugged out of her day dress and laid it on her bed before slipping into her new white silk. She put on her matching slippers and joined her sisters in Anne's room, which was the largest and had the best light. They helped each other with ribbons and flowers and took turns in front of Anne's mirror. They had done this a hundred times before, but tonight there was a buzz of excitement in the room that was entirely new.

"Sit *still*," Anne told Sophie, who was fidgeting in the chair so much that the hairpins and carnations were going in crooked. Once the pins were in, Anne took the loose, light brown hair that framed Sophie's face and wrapped it around her index finger, breathed a spell-word, and released the hair, now a perfect curl. She repeated the process until Sophie's face was framed by six perfect ringlets, which somehow made her blue eyes look bigger. Then Anne rested her hand lightly on the top of Sophie's head and whispered another word. She dropped her hand with a sigh. "Good. It will stay up all night, no matter how energetically you dance."

I wish I had a spell to make my hair hold a curl...

Eleanor, who had been watching them in the mirror, caught Anne's eye and winked. She looked back at her own reflection

CHAPTER 1

and bit her lip as she twisted her darker brown hair tighter and adjusted the pins. She and Anne always curled their hair by magic, but they never needed the spell to keep the rest of it in place.

When they were all ready, they stood for a moment together in the gathering dark in Anne's room. Anne and Eleanor were of a height, not tall but not petite, and willowy. Sophie was a few inches shorter with light, girlish curves.

"It will be fine," Eleanor said, as much to reassure herself as her older sister.

"Better than fine," Sophie added. "It's not dancing with *her*, but it's still dancing."

We see who "she" is later in the book.

A moment later, they were informed that the carriage was at the door. They bundled themselves up in furs and capes and joined their father and aunt to climb into the carriage. Lady Sterling's residence was not far, and despite the press of traffic, they were pulling to a stop before Eleanor even felt like she'd settled into her seat.

They'd visited Lady Sterling before, so the house itself wasn't overwhelming, but they'd never seen her ballroom. It was already crowded when they entered. Eleanor swallowed back a gasp. There had to be a hundred couples here, nearly double the number that attended their most popular balls at

Fairfield Hall. And the room itself, with marble floors and pale wallpaper and gold trim, was nearly large enough to hold them all.

Lady Elizabeth Cole, Countess of Sterling, greeted them at the door. Father bowed; Aunt Everley curtsied, and Eleanor and her sisters followed suit.

"Sir William Maybury, Lady Everley, welcome," Lady Sterling said, extending a hand to each of them. "Miss Maybury, Miss Eleanor, and Miss Sophie, so good to see you here."

The oldest daughter always went by Miss Last-name, and the younger sisters were Miss First-name. So Anne is Miss Maybury as the eldest.

"Thank you for your hospitality," Anne said. "We've been so looking forward to it."

"As have I, to be sure," Lady Sterling said. "Please allow me to introduce my son, George Cole."

The young man at her side had curling red-gold hair like his mother's and freckles across his nose. His coat was a dark turquoise that brightened his blue eyes. He bowed and smiled brightly at Anne. "Would you honor me with the first set, Miss Maybury?"

Anne accepted graciously.

Lady Sterling was barely attending. "Where is…" She looked around. "James, dear—oh, there you are." Another young man had appeared beside the first. His appearance was entirely different: tall, dark hair, dark eyes, an aquiline nose. His expression was serious but for a slight quirk at the corner of his mouth. His own impeccably tailored coat was a somber dark blue over a burgundy waistcoat. "May I also introduce my cousin, Mr. James Weston, magician to the Royal Navy."

I'm pretty sure his resemblance to Matthew Macfadyen from the 2005 *Pride and Prejudice* movie is unintentional. Or at least subconscious.

Mr. Weston bowed. Eleanor curtsied with the rest, and as she rose, she just caught a significant look that passed to Mr. Weston from Lady Sterling. His mouth quirked a bit more.

The music was starting up as he said, "Miss Eleanor, may I have the first set?"

Eleanor nodded and took his arm, following Mr. Cole and her sister. Once out of earshot of Aunt Everley, she said, "You needn't ask me if you're not inclined to dance. I won't be offended."

Mr. Weston looked at her, surprised. His mouth quirked again. "I confess, Miss Maybury, that I'm rarely inclined to dance. I am not the most graceful dancer, and I'd hate for you to form a first impression of me based on it."

Eleanor opened her mouth to speak, but he forestalled her. "I have, however, promised Lady Sterling that I would dance at least once tonight, and you're as lovely a partner as a man could ask for."

Eleanor blushed. "Are you hoping flattery will gain you a better first impression?"

"It can hardly hurt."

They joined the dance. Eleanor did not think Mr. Weston nearly as ungraceful as he had suggested, but she couldn't help noticing that he moved with a slight limp. As the dance brought them close to each other again, Mr. Weston asked, "Have you but lately come to town?"

In the original fairy tale, the hero is an old war veteran. James isn't exactly old, but he does have his war wound.

"We've been here these two weeks, but this is the first ball we've attended."

"And is it your first visit to London?"

"We stayed with my aunt at Christmas once or twice when I was young."

"Which might as well mean yes," Mr. Weston said. "How much have you seen since your arrival?"

"Can one see anything in all this smoke and fog?" Eleanor said. "I don't remember London being so dirty." They parted for a moment before coming back together. "But, of course, that's not what you meant. We've been to one play—*The Tempest*—and spent nearly all the rest of the time at the

CHAPTER 1

modiste's getting fitted up for the Season."

These are pretty standard questions to ask on a first meeting in a ballroom, at least if you're in a Jane Austen book.

"Ah," Mr. Weston said knowingly. "New clothes are always the first priority on entering town. I myself always need a new coat or cravat to feel properly ready to face Society."

The set ended. As they left the floor, Eleanor said, "You misled me, Mr. Weston. You were no more awkward than any other dancer. It is only too crowded for anyone to appear at their best."

"I am sure that is not true of you, Miss Eleanor," Mr. Weston said gallantly. "But believe that, by all means."

He escorted Eleanor back to Aunt Everley, bowed, and disappeared back into the crowd. Eleanor could see Sophie changing partners, and Anne was talking with a young lady at the edge of the dance floor.

"He seems a charming young man," Aunt Everley said, looking after Mr. Weston. "Lady Sterling told me that he's six- or seven-and-twenty, and he has no family, so she's half adopted him. He has an estate in Hertfordshire worth upwards of three thousand pounds a year and has spent the last seven years at sea serving as a magician aboard the—oh, what ship did she say?"

What good is gossip if you can't get all the private personal details, like what his income is??

They were interrupted by an acquaintance, and introduction followed introduction for the rest of the set, as Aunt Everley was acquainted with at least half the room. Eleanor soon tired of curtsying every few minutes, but it ended with her being engaged for the next four sets. Her sisters were engaged as well, and they passed each other in the dance. The lively country dances put Eleanor more at ease than anything else in that grand, crowded ballroom could do. Her final partner escorted her to the refreshments, where she met Anne, and he left them drinking punch together.

After a moment, Eleanor said, "I told you it would be fine."

At home, Anne might have made a face or rolled her eyes, but not in Lady Sterling's ballroom. She merely smiled, eyes sparkling, and sipped her drink.

"It would be if it were not so stifling in here."

Eleanor took her sister's hand and led her through the crowd to the nearest window. It was closed against the chill of a March evening, but Eleanor lifted the sash a few inches.

"*Now* it's fine," she said.

"Miss Eleanor."

Eleanor whirled around. If her glass hadn't been almost empty, she would have spilled it over Anne. Her cheeks glowed.

"Forgive me for startling you," Mr. Weston said, mouth twitching. "May I have the next set?"

"I thought you only promised Lady Sterling to dance once," she blurted before she collected herself. Anne stepped on her foot. She blushed brighter.

"At *least* once," he corrected. "And as you didn't seem to mind my dancing before, I thought perhaps you would tolerate it again. Unless, of course, you were telling a kind falsehood earlier."

"No, not at all," Eleanor said quickly. "I'd be happy to dance. You simply caught me by surprise."

"And in the heinous act of opening a window, no less." His mock solemnity was too much. Eleanor giggled. Anne reached over and took the punch glass from her hand, and Eleanor took Mr. Weston's arm to join the dance again.

Mr. James Weston called on George Cole and his mother late the following morning. Lady Sterling had told him never to stand on ceremony and to treat their home as his own, but this morning he waited until well past the beginning of visiting hours. The ball had gone late the previous night, and Lady Sterling had had to farewell all of her many guests. It was only to be expected that she would sleep in and breakfast late. James had been up and pacing his own rooms for hours. He hadn't attended many balls since returning to England, and he could never remember feeling so alive the next morning. He intended to convince George to go with him to the club: a little fencing match was just what he needed.

He was ushered into the drawing room. George lounged in a chair, hiding his yawn behind a book. Lady Sterling looked as elegant and unfatigued as ever. James greeted them both and sat in a chair near his friend, but, as so many times already this morning, the memory of Miss Eleanor Maybury's giggle brought him back to his feet to walk about the room.

"You're limping more than usual," George said bluntly, watching him.

"I'm not in the habit of dancing," James said.

"No indeed," Lady Sterling agreed. "You've been at sea too long and have forgotten a good many things."

"I haven't forgotten *how* to dance," James protested.

"No, dear," said Lady Sterling. "But when you promised me to dance at least once, you were supposed to dance with more than one young lady, not twice with the same one."

James colored and began another lap around the room.

"Well then, mother," George said. "Weston won't ask it, so I will. What do you know of the Mayburys?"

"Sir William Maybury is a well-respected baronet," she said. "His sister, Dowager Lady Everley, was married to the late Lord Everley of Sussex, and Sir William's son Charles inherited his uncle's title. Sir William's own wife passed away several years ago, and his daughters have been managing his home ever since."

"And this is their first Season?" George asked.

"Yes. Lady Everley wanted to bring Miss Maybury to town years ago, but first it was too soon after her mother's death, and then she refused to come without her sisters."

CHAPTER 1

"How odd."

"Indeed. I understand that they were also waiting for their youngest brother to be old enough for school."

James listened to the conversation attentively as he paced the room. The closeness of the sisters was charming, and he saw nothing wrong with them waiting to come out until their youngest brother was out of their care.

"And what are their accomplishments?" George asked, giving James a look that said he really ought to begin asking questions himself if he wanted to hear the answers so badly.

"Playing, singing, magic, and French," Lady Sterling said. "Miss Sophie also reads Greek."

"Magic?" James asked, joining the conversation for the first time.

"Particularly Miss Eleanor, I believe," Lady Sterling said. "Which adds to her other charms, don't you think?" She raised a delicately arched eyebrow.

Well, yes. Yes, it does. Especially to a man who has devoted his life to magic.

"I hardly think so." George scratched his freckled nose. "So many young ladies can do magic; it's as common as playing the pianoforte."

"Quite," his mother said, amused. "Now, James, dear, did you come see us because you were bored at home, or did you have another purpose beyond *not* asking me about Miss Eleanor Maybury?"

"Do I need a reason to visit you, madam?"

"Of course not, dear." She looked at him expectantly.

"As it happens, I am intending to go to the club, and I thought to force Cole, here, to come with me."

"Excellent." Lady Sterling smiled. "Off with you both. I have letters to attend to."

George sighed and set his book on the table. James grinned at him.

"You owe me a drink after all this," George muttered as they climbed into the carriage that would take them to Pall Mall.

"Naturally," James agreed.

George yawned ostentatiously the whole way to the club. James ignored him. They didn't speak until they had retrieved their fencing gear and were removing their coats and waistcoats.

"All right, Weston, out with it already," George burst. "You like her."

James felt a smile pulling at the corners of his mouth, but he continued to methodically untie his cravat. "She's interesting," he said finally. "Surprising. Not like all the insipid beauties who can't think for themselves."

"You mean half the *ton*."

"Indeed. And her eyes. They're stormy gray but with flecks of silver that put me in mind of... waterfalls." He frowned down at his hands.

CHAPTER 1

There's a reason for her waterfall-silver eyes...

George chuckled. "It's a bit soon to be writing her poetry, isn't it?"

James threw a mask at him, which George only just caught.

"If you like her so much," George grumbled, "why aren't you in her drawing room right now instead of bothering me?"

"Because I don't want her to associate me with the overeager puppies who will be fawning on them today," James said. "And with three young ladies making their debut at once, they're sure to have an abundance of visitors. I wouldn't even get a chance to talk to her."

George frowned at him. "You've put more thought into this than I ever have."

I considered giving George Cole the role of Prince Charming in a Cinderella retelling (with Eleanor as the fairy godmother), but the rest of the story never fell into place.

"I've been up since dawn." James pulled his mask over his face. "I've had time to think."

George shook his head and pulled his own mask on. "Well, it's a long season. I expect you'll see her often enough to get your fill of those waterfall eyes."

James wished he hadn't said anything. He raised his foil and determined to show his friend no mercy.

It was a good thing Aunt Everley's drawing room was so large, Eleanor thought as more and more callers arrived. Aunt Everley had warned them that the first morning after their entrance to Society would be like this, but Eleanor hadn't quite believed her. But seeing eight young men in the drawing room at once, most of whom had brought flowers and all of whom were trying to solicit the attention of one of the sisters, proved that her aunt knew what she was talking about.

Half of the gentlemen were unabashedly there to see Anne. Sophie had one particular admirer, and so did Eleanor, and two others seemed eager to make themselves agreeable to everyone. Eleanor couldn't figure out why they would come calling if they couldn't even decide which sister they preferred, but it was helpful that some of the gathering were willing to make conversation with whoever was next to them. One of Anne's admirers, disgruntled at being so far from where she was seated, kept leaning around the gentleman beside him and trying to join her conversation, though he couldn't hear half of what was being said. Eleanor bit her lip once or twice to keep from laughing, and sobered quickly at a look from Aunt Everley. She wouldn't discourage any of Anne's suitors, however ridiculous.

CHAPTER 1

It was an exhausting morning, and by the time the last gentleman took his leave and Aunt Everley told Harvey, the head footman, to have tea sent up and admit no more visitors, Eleanor had had enough of polite, disinterested conversation for a month. She leaned back in her chair, closed her eyes, and found herself the slightest bit disappointed. It had been a most successful morning, evidencing a most successful entrance into Society, according to Aunt Everley. <u>But Eleanor had rather hoped that Mr. Weston would call that morning.</u> He had danced with her twice, after all. But then, he had been dancing out of obligation, and that she was his choice to fulfill that obligation meant nothing. Still, he had been interesting, and he was a magician, and she would have liked to talk to him again. Not that they would have been able to talk about more than the weather and last night's ball in a gathering such as this morning's had been. Eleanor sighed and sat up to take tea with the family, putting her disappointment behind her.

I had a massive crush on my husband within the first twenty-four (or four-and-twenty) hours of meeting him, so crush-at-first-sight is something I resonate with.

Chapter 2

That Saturday morning, Aunt Everley's drawing room had a constant stream of visitors. Between the interruptions and her internal tension, Eleanor had given up on any hope of accomplishing anything. Anne was knitting a shawl in dark rose wool, and her hands worked quickly while she smiled and chatted politely with their guests.

Anytime I can have my characters knit, I do. Yarn is my other obsession. And her shawl is one of my favorite colors.

Eleanor was supposed to be embroidering something that might become a cover for the pianoforte stool, but she was barely paying attention to what her needle was doing. She was somewhat more occupied in watching Sophie's progress on her filigree box. But even that couldn't occupy her for long.

Tonight was Seventh Night.

CHAPTER 2

They'd had to skip the last two, due to their arrival and settling into the house in London. But it was time to go again, and there was no talk of missing another. Eleanor could sense the excitement bottled up inside Sophie. She was always the most eager and the least concerned about logistics. Anne's composure was so complete that even Eleanor couldn't tell if she was nervous. Eleanor certainly was. They had always been in their own home, with their own family, able to arrange their engagements as they wished. Now, however, they were in Aunt Everley's home, and *she* was the one in charge of their schedule. And tonight they were engaged to go to a card party that would likely end late.

Eleanor still hadn't figured out a satisfactory way of keeping them all at home by the time they were upstairs in Anne's room, dressing to go out.

"You'll have to have a headache tonight," Anne told Eleanor.

"Me?"

"Well, it can't be Sophie," Anne said. "She's too lively today. And if *I* have a headache, you'll give away the lie."

"You *are* a terrible liar, Eleanor," Sophie agreed.

Me too. Not that I've made a habit of practicing, but I'm definitely not a good liar.

Eleanor didn't think it was such a bad thing to be truthful, but at times it was inconvenient. "Then is it wise for me to put on an act in front of an entire evening party? Couldn't I convince Aunt Everley during dinner, before we go?"

"But if you're unwell *before* the party, she'll make you stay home to rest alone," Anne said, twisting her hair up. "Besides, you've already made it clear that you find the heat and... odor of the crowded London parties to be a bit much. It would be perfectly reasonable for you to develop a headache at one."

Much as it pains me to admit that the Regency period was not all glitz and glam, the prevailing hygiene practices sucked. Baths were rare (like, monthly, although washing oneself daily, without a full bath, was becoming more popular among the wealthy), and toothpaste wasn't what it is today. Now picture an enclosed space crowded with people.

Eleanor had to admit Anne's logic, though she kept trying to come up with a better plan. She couldn't, and they went. They arrived in the Harris's drawing room after dinner as the card tables were being arranged. Papa and Aunt Everley sat down to whist with Mr. Weston and Mr. Harris. Eleanor sat between her sisters to play casino. The room was every bit as hot and crowded as Eleanor could wish; much more than was comfortable; perfect for bringing on a headache.

During the first hour, she sighed occasionally and frowned, fanned herself, and gave one of her sisters a weak smile, as if to reassure them that she was fine. During the second hour, her hand went to her temple several times, and she lost track of her turn. Sophie had to remind her of what she was supposed to be doing. At last, she turned to Anne.

"It's time," Eleanor whispered.

Anne nodded and put a comforting arm around her. "Rest your head in your hand," she murmured. "I'll go tell Papa and Aunt."

Eleanor did, resting her elbow on the table and her forehead in her hand, mindless of her cards and what was going on in the game. Sophie gave Eleanor all her attention while it wasn't her turn, and even spared her the trouble of answering the polite inquiries from around the table, assuring everyone that it was just a headache.

Anne came back. Eleanor glanced at the whist table. Aunt Everley ordered the carriage, and they finished their game while waiting for it. Papa glanced at his daughters several times. Eleanor could feel her face going hot. Her hands felt clammy. She fanned herself absently. At last the carriage was announced, and Anne assisted Eleanor to her feet. Eleanor took her sister's arm and followed her father and aunt to the door, with Sophie bringing up the rear. As they passed the whist table, Eleanor noticed that <u>Mr. Weston's eyes were turned their way</u>. His expression was as serious as ever. She turned her head away, toward Anne, hiding her burning cheeks. She had a sudden irrational fear that he could see through her deception. But why should he, when no one else did? Regardless, Eleanor had a sick feeling in her stomach that he should witness her lying.

"We'll be home soon," Anne murmured once they were in the carriage, giving Eleanor's hand a squeeze.

"You look very flushed, dear," Aunt Everley said. "Why didn't you say something sooner?"

"Everyone was having such a pleasant time," Eleanor said weakly.

"Nonsense," Papa told her. "If you feel unwell, you must tell us at once. You are not accustomed yet to the constant social events and late nights. It can be overwhelming when you're used to country life."

Eleanor simply nodded, wishing her palms would stop sweating through her silk gloves.

Once at home, her sisters escorted her to her room and put her straight to bed without undressing. Eleanor made a show of flinching as the grandfather clock in the drawing room chimed half past nine, as if the deep, resounding gong hurt her head.

Aunt Everley stopped at the door as Anne unpinned Eleanor's hair for her and began to braid it loosely.

"We'll sit with her, Aunt," Anne said.

"We'll be quiet," Sophie assured her. "Unless Eleanor would like me to read to her."

"Greek poetry does put me to sleep," Eleanor said.

Sophie glared at her but said nothing.

"Use a cool cloth for her head," Aunt Everley advised. "Have you a spell for the pain?"

"Not a good one," Eleanor mumbled.

A few minutes later, Papa came to wish her goodnight. "Call if you need anything," he said.

They waited together in silence for several long minutes. At length, Anne walked to the door, peered out, then closed it softly. She whispered a word and turned back to her sisters.

Eleanor sat up. "I'll open the gate. Sophie, can you do the

chronology spell while Anne helps me with my hair?"

Sophie nodded and began pacing around the edges of the room, muttering as she went.

Eleanor coiled her braid into a bun, which Anne secured with hairpins.

"He'll be able to tell which of us feigned illness tonight," Anne said with a sigh. She handed Eleanor her shoes.

"Yes, but who knew that Eleanor's discomfort would look just like the symptoms of a headache?" Sophie said. "She was more convincing than I expected."

Eleanor blushed and led the way to the huge wardrobe that took up one corner of the room. She put her hand on the knob, concentrated hard on the spell-word, and turned. Instead of opening onto the interior of a wardrobe hung with gowns, the open door revealed a staircase that descended away from them. Small silver lanterns hung from tall columns every few yards and made the pale marble glow. The air coming through the doorway was much warmer than that of a chill March night. Sophie bounced on her toes with glee, but she waited for Eleanor to go first. Once they were all through the gate, Anne pulled the door shut behind them. They took hands and skipped lightly down the three dozen steps to where the passage leveled out. The walk from here took half an hour. The sameness of the marble and columns and lanterns and silence would have gotten tedious if they hadn't known what awaited them at the end.

Music was the first sign that they were getting close. It began so faintly that Eleanor didn't know when she began to hear it, but she felt it in her veins before she recognized it with her ears. Soon it echoed through the passage. The murmur of voices soon became audible as well: talking, laughing, singing, calling. Sophie was in front now, half dragging her sisters, one by each hand. The girls began laughing now, too. It was impossible not to. Sophie's excitement was contagious, and even Eleanor almost forgot the unpleasant taste of untruth.

The passage ended abruptly, spilling them out into a broad, open colonnade. Refreshments on silver platters were piled on stone tables and low columns. Tall, gracious figures gathered around the platters. Another cluster of beautiful people were assembled at the other end of the colonnade. Eleanor and her sisters made for this group. As they approached, elegant ladies and gentlemen stepped aside to let them pass. At last they reached *her*: the Faerie Queen herself. She sat on a marble throne, wearing a dress as pale as the stone. It was not so totally different from the muslin that Eleanor wore, except that the neck was wide and low, and it had no sleeves. It might have been made of silk; it might have been woven of spider webs and moonlight. The Queen beckoned the girls closer with one ungloved hand. Her olive skin was flawless. Her hair, dark as a moonless night, was pulled up in unruly but somehow perfect curls.

"Welcome, children," she said. Her voice was low and musical, and her dark eyes sparkled.

Eleanor let go of Sophie's hand and curtsied. "Thank you, Your Majesty," she said.

"It has been long enough since you've joined us," the Queen said. "I will not detain you from the dance." She dismissed them with a wave.

Sophie led the way back through the crowd to the end of the colonnade where the stone stopped abruptly and a broad, green meadow stretched out. This meadow was already a mass of twirling couples. The musicians were off to the left, near the colonnade.

"*This* is what a ball should be," Sophie said.

"Outdoors and with space to move," Anne agreed.

A tall gentleman broke away from the crowd of dancers, approached them, and bowed. His hair was dark, straight, and long, tied back at the nape of his neck. His eyes gleamed silver like a stream in the sun. He was as ageless as the Queen, as young as spring and as ancient as centuries.

"Welcome, children," he said warmly. "It is good to see you here again."

Eleanor suppressed an irritated sigh. She hated that everyone here called them children. It wasn't condescension—the Fae simply saw their visitors that way. Perhaps they *had* been little more than children when they'd first been invited to come, five years ago. But Eleanor said nothing. They were only allowed to visit as children.

That was one of the primary rules of their visits to Seventh Night: once they were engaged, they couldn't return.

She curtsied with her sisters. "Lord River," she murmured.

Lord River was not his real name, of course. Faeries never gave out their true names. But it was what Mama had called him, and he allowed Eleanor and her sisters to call him that as well. It was he who had come to them that evening, three months after Mama had died, and shown them how to open the gate, and brought them to Faerie for their first ball. He had been the first to greet them at the dancing every Seventh Night since.

"You have lately gone to London," he said. "Are you settled?"

Anne gave a brief answer. As she finished, two other gentlemen left the dancers. They bowed and held out their hands to Sophie and Anne, who curtsied to Lord River and went with them. Eleanor didn't recognize the gentlemen, but she rarely did. There were so many people here it was impossible to keep track of them all, and she suspected them of changing their appearances as often as fine ladies changed gowns. But Lord River was always the same, and now he held out his hand to lead Eleanor to the dance.

A waltz struck up just as they reached the center of the meadow. The music felt like its own form of magic, sweeping her into its motion so that her pulse kept time with the rhythm and her feet itched to move. Even if one didn't like dancing—and Eleanor and her sisters absolutely did—one would be drawn in and enjoy every minute.

Lord River put his free hand on Eleanor's waist and guided her into the dance, both of them twirling in perfect sync. She knew before he spoke that Anne's prediction was correct and she'd been singled out for a reason.

"You were indisposed this evening," he said. "I trust you feel better now?"

"It was nothing," she said, politely and dismissively. His silver eyes held hers. She blushed. "If we had not left the party, we could not have come here tonight."

"Could you not have opened a gate at the party? Any doorway will do."

"No," Eleanor said. "We would have been missed."

Lord River was silent for a long moment. Eleanor tried to enjoy the dance—all the Fae were exceptional dancers—but her stomach was knotted, and her cheeks were still hot.

"It would be wise for you to choose truth in all your dealings, Eleanor."

CHAPTER 2

Good advice for all of us. (Although a little hypocritical, which we'll see later.)

Lord River's words stung. She hadn't actually spoken a lie, and it had only been done at her sisters' urging. "Why are you reprimanding me alone?" she asked. "My sisters are complicit as well."

"I am not reprimanding," Lord River said mildly. "And their choices are their own. *You* are responsible for *yours*." He led her through a complicated turn. "Was it worth it?"

Eleanor could see her sister's joyful faces as they twirled with their partners. Her sisters were worth everything. "Yes," she said. Suddenly, she remembered the feeling of Mr. Weston's eyes on her. "This time."

"But perhaps not another?"

Eleanor sighed. "Perhaps not."

"Remember that," Lord River said as the dance ended.

Eleanor thanked him automatically. Another gentleman claimed her hand for a country dance, and then another. She danced for an hour, giddily carried by the music and the joy of the dance, before she saw another familiar face. Lady Snow stood apart, not among the dancers but also not in the group around Her Majesty. Eleanor politely declined joining the circle dance and made her way to the lady. Lady Snow had been another of Mama's particular friends. She was lithe and graceful, dressed in pure white silk dotted with icy diamonds. Her hair was white, too, though not from old age. She smiled at Eleanor and took her hand, and together they walked to the refreshments.

"Have you planned your exhibition spells?" Lady Snow asked.

"I have an idea or two," Eleanor said, accepting a crystalline glass of water. She eyed the colorful *hors d'oeuvres* on the trays, but didn't touch. That was another rule: eating the food would trap them in Faerie forever. "I think Sophie has had a much easier time picking songs to perfect on the pianoforte."

During the social Season in London, young ladies would have opportunities to showcase their skills (generally musical) at various private parties as part of the evening's entertainment. Jane Austen included several of these events in her books. In my Regency England, magic is also an acceptable accomplishment to display.

The Faerie's eyes were the pale blue of shadows on snow. "Perhaps. Which were you thinking?"

"The violets, the rose bouquet, and the rainbow." They stood for some time discussing spells and illusions before they were called back to the dance.

Eleanor's mind was full as the last dance ended. She couldn't stop smiling any more than Sophie or Anne could, but she was ready to say her farewell to Her Majesty and walk back up the passage to her room. She shivered in the cold chamber when they all climbed through the wardrobe door. Closing it behind her, she felt the spell fade. Sophie walked around the room and murmured a single word to end her chronology spell. Before Anne took her lock off the door, though, the three of them sat down on the edge of Eleanor's bed and took off their shoes. The leather and silk were frayed and worn from the long night of dancing and the walk there and back. Eleanor said the spell-word in her mind as her sisters whispered it beside her. They watched the shoes repair themselves, becoming like new again.

Unlike in the original fairy tale, the girls can repair their shoes so that their secret isn't discovered.

Anne opened the door and peeked out. She nodded at Sophie, who slipped quietly out and down the hall to her room. Anne stayed behind to help Eleanor unpin her hair and remove her gown. Then Anne, too, crept from the room. As Eleanor closed the door behind her, she heard the grandfather clock in the drawing room strike ten. She felt a little thrill at the confirmation that the chronology spell had worked. Her bedchamber, while the spell was on it, had been taken out of the flow of time, hours passing within while minutes passed outside.

Eleanor got into bed for the second time that night. She

lay awake for a long time, her feelings in a jumble. She felt the joy and rush of dancing, the persistent awe of Her Majesty, the enthusiasm of discussing magic with Lady Snow, the reproach from Lord River. Mama had always impressed on them the importance of honesty and integrity. But Mama had also impressed on them the importance of keeping Faerie, and their connection with it, secret. How were they going to last the Season in London with a secret that took them from home every Saturday night?

Chapter 3

Eleanor woke late the following morning, only just in time to eat a quick breakfast before dressing for church.

"We would have let you sleep," Aunt Everley said. "How are you feeling this morning?"

"Perfectly well," Eleanor assured her. "Only tired." And hungry. Magic used energy just like any other form of exertion, requiring food, water, and sleep to recover. As long as each of them only maintained one of the spells, the sisters could wait until breakfast the next morning, but they were usually famished by then.

Aunt Everley nodded. "Your father told me last night of your family tradition of not making or receiving social calls on Sundays. Given how unused to so busy a social schedule you are, I have agreed to keep this tradition while you are staying with me. I will also limit our evening engagements to four a week so that we may all be sure of adequate rest."

"Thank you, Aunt," Eleanor said with real gratitude. She hoped that many of those evenings at home would be Saturday evenings.

When they returned from church, Aunt Everley told the footman to refuse all visitors. The family spent the afternoon in the sitting room. Papa read to them as Anne knit, Aunt

Everley sewed, and Eleanor practiced the rainbow spell she'd discussed with Lady Snow. The spell involved taking a cup of water, suspending the droplets in air, and illuminating them all at once.

"That is a lovely rainbow, dear," her aunt said after half an hour. "But must you make it so wet inside? <u>Isn't there rain enough outside?</u>"

It does rain a lot in England. I've only visited a couple times, but I remember the rain.

Eleanor apologized and returned the water to the cup.

She turned her attention to Sophie, who was practicing a new Italian song on the pianoforte. The music was beautiful, but Sophie had to keep asking Papa to pause and help her with the pronunciation.

"Why don't they write songs in Greek?" Sophie demanded in frustration.

Nobody answered. It was best not to bother Sophie with logic or reason when she was in a mood. Anne just smiled, and Aunt Everley called for tea.

CHAPTER 3

They were engaged for most of the week with dinners and evening parties that Aunt Everley had already accepted invitations to. Eleanor didn't mind the evening parties, though, because the weather was so wet and drab that it kept everyone home during the day. Thursday, however, dawned fine and sunny, and the ladies of the house walked out to enjoy it. Down the street to Portman Square and on to Hyde Park, where half the town seemed to have the same idea. Their progress was stopped every few minutes to greet acquaintances.

A chunk of my research for this book consisted of rereading Jane Austen's books (I know, hardest research ever, right?) and paying close attention to locations (Portman Square was in *Sense and Sensibility*, I think) and comparing those to maps of London.

Not far into the park, they crossed paths with a friend of Aunt Everley's, Mrs. Graham, and her daughter. The two ladies turned to walk with them. Miss Graham was a pretty but solemn girl of three-and-twenty, and she and Anne struck up a conversation while the older ladies did the same. This left Sophie and Eleanor to walk happily together. Sophie paused to admire the buds on every tree and notice the shoots of all the hyacinths. Eleanor acknowledged her sister's remarks but soon grew bored and began to watch the people parading through the park. She noticed two gentlemen coming along an adjoining path. She couldn't see their faces, but they were talking animatedly. On noticing them, one of the gentlemen took his leave of the other and approached them. As he came, Eleanor noticed that he was limping, and she recognized him just a moment before he bowed to her aunt.

"Mr. Weston, how good to see you!" Aunt Everley said. "May I introduce my friend, Mrs. Graham, and her daughter? This is Mr. Weston, a magician and a cousin of Lady Sterling's."

Mr. Weston bowed again and requested to join their party. Aunt Everley agreed readily, and Mr. Weston fell in to walk beside Eleanor and Sophie.

"You're looking well, Miss Eleanor," he said. "I trust you are feeling better?"

The last time they'd seen Mr. Weston was the evening of the false headache. "I'm feeling very well today," she assured him. "The headache of last Saturday was nothing, really."

"I'm glad to hear it," he said. "I'm surprised residents of London don't have headaches every day—it is so crowded and smoky here."

"Do you not like town?" asked Eleanor.

"I prefer open spaces," he admitted. "After seven years at sea, and most of my life in country houses, I find town somewhat oppressive."

"So do I," Sophie agreed. "Is it business that brings you to town, if you'd rather be in the country?"

"Sophie!" Eleanor hissed. Her sister had not yet learned to control the urge to pry into other people's affairs.

A smile twitched at the corner of Mr. Weston's mouth. "A perfectly reasonable question," he said. "My friend Cole promised Lady Sterling to spend the Season with her, and he insisted that I come too. He seems to think I've been away

CHAPTER 3

from Society for too long."

They walked in silence for a moment, before Eleanor observed the first daffodils. This introduced the subject of flowers and fine weather. Eleanor couldn't help but notice that Mr. Weston's limp was significantly worse than it had been the previous week at Lady Sterling's ball.

After several minutes, Eleanor's curiosity was too much to bear, and she couldn't resist the urge to pry either. "Please forgive the impertinence, Mr. Weston, but I must ask: did you receive a wound in your time at sea?"

Mr. Weston colored slightly and looked down at his left leg. "I did, Miss Eleanor, and as you see, it still pains me at times, particularly after rain such as we have had recently."

"Could magic not have prevented it?" Sophie asked.

"The rain? Or the ball from a pistol catching me just above the knee?" he said.

Eleanor began to wish she hadn't brought up the subject. Mr. Weston seemed perfectly cheerful and willing to talk, however.

"Oh, I know one can't prevent the rain," Sophie said. "Nor even delay it for long."

"Could magic have prevented the injury, then?" Mr. Weston said. "Possibly. But at the time, my attention and spells were focused on protecting the crew and keeping the ship afloat. I didn't see the man with the pistol until it was too late."

"Oh," Sophie said.

"Magic *did* keep me from losing the leg," Mr. Weston added. "But this is hardly suitable conversation for young ladies."

"But were you able to save the ship?" Eleanor asked.

"With help, yes," Mr. Weston said, with a quirk at the corner of his mouth.

Eleanor wanted to ask more about such sea adventures, but

at that moment, Mrs. Graham and her daughter made their goodbyes and left. Aunt Everley and Anne now joined the conversation.

"Do you have any plans now that you're back in the country, Mr. Weston?" Aunt Everley asked.

"Nothing decided," he said. "I'd like to do something useful, but I haven't found anything to suit yet. After seven years of service to king and country, I want something active and of practical importance."

"Something with magic?" Anne asked.

"Yes," he said.

"I'd like to hear, sometime, about the magic you've done," Eleanor said. "I don't often get to meet a practicing magician."

"Please don't start her talking about magic," Sophie groaned. "She won't stop for hours."

Eleanor blushed and made a face at her sister. "I could say the same about your Greek poets," she shot back.

"Girls," Aunt Everley said reprovingly.

At that moment, a young man walking the opposite way gave a start and exclaimed, "Weston! Is that you? It's been years!"

Mr. Weston excused himself to speak to the gentleman. The ladies studied the newcomer. He was not tall, but he was dressed with simple elegance and carried himself confidently. He had a round, cheerful face and an easy smile. Mr. Weston soon brought him over to them and introduced him as Mr. John Farrow.

"We were at Oxford together," Mr. Weston explained.

"It's a pleasure to meet you, Mr. Farrow," Aunt Everley said.

"The pleasure is mine." Mr. Farrow bowed.

"Are you a magician too?" Eleanor asked.

"Not at all," he said easily. "I never had an aptitude for it. I'm the curate of a parish in Essex."

"Indeed," Aunt Everley said. They began to speak of people and places in the county, as Aunt Everley had lived for many years near Halstead. Before long, they were back at the entrance of the park, and the party divided. The ladies walked home, all well satisfied with their outing.

At breakfast the next morning, Anne looked up eagerly when Harvey, the footman, brought the day's post. Several invitations were set before Aunt Everley, and a business letter for Papa, but nothing for the girls.

"Were you expecting a letter?" Papa asked.

"No," Anne sighed. "I was only hoping to hear from Henry. He's been at Mr. Smith's for several months now, you know, and I haven't heard from him."

"A boy of eleven will hardly write often to his sister," Aunt Everley said, glancing over the invitations.

"No, I know," Anne said. "And Charles isn't a good example for him as to how to maintain a correspondence. Have you heard from Charles lately, Papa?"

"About a month ago," Papa said, "before we came to London. He wrote that both he and Henry were well. I don't expect to hear from him again for another two or three months."

I included the two brothers (who never actually appear on the page) partly for the family dynamics but also to give a valid reason for Anne to have delayed her debut so that all three could be coming out at the same time. Anything less than care for Henry would have been overruled by Aunt Everley.

Anne frowned at her plate. "Well, I suppose that it won't hurt if *I* write to Henry. A boy may not choose to write to his sisters, but his sisters may write to him, and it may do away with any homesickness he might be feeling."

She got up to leave the table.

"When you're finished your letter, dear, I would like to discuss our dinner party," Aunt Everley said.

"What dinner party?" Eleanor asked.

"The first of several that we shall host this season," Aunt Everley said. She frowned at Eleanor and Sophie. "Did you think that all our evenings would be spent out on the town? *Someone* must host."

Eleanor met Sophie's wide eyes. "I hadn't actually thought about it," Eleanor admitted. "All the newness of being in town made the reciprocity of hosting slip my mind."

Sophie nodded.

Papa chuckled and got up. "Being in town can make a lot of things slip one's mind until one is used to it. Enjoy your planning. I'm off to meet Lord Rupert at the club."

He left, and Anne went to the sitting room to write her letter. Eleanor finished her breakfast and followed her. She'd left her copy of *Ford's* upstairs; she'd purchased a new book of illusions at Hatchard's soon after arriving in town, and now she took it with her to a seat by the window. If they were to have a dinner party, Aunt Everley was sure to expect the girls to entertain their guests with their accomplishments. Sophie would play and sing, and Anne, if she wasn't too busy playing hostess, would choose either to play the pianoforte like Sophie or do magic. It was never a question with Eleanor: she always did magic. It was just a matter of choosing which spell would make the biggest splash with a London audience.

She was distracted by Harvey opening the door to announce visitors in the drawing room, and she was more than surprised to hear that it was Mr. Weston and his friend, Mr. Farrow. Eleanor got up to join them.

Anne lingered at the writing desk. "I'll be there in a moment," she said. "I'm nearly done my letter."

Eleanor nodded and rested her hand on her sister's shoulder as she passed. "Give Henry my love," she said.

The gentlemen rose as she entered the drawing room. Aunt Everley and Sophie were already there, and a maid arrived on Eleanor's heels with the tea service. Eleanor curtsied and took a seat, excusing Anne as she did so.

"She's finishing a letter to our youngest brother, Henry," she said. "He's recently gone to be educated in the home of a private gentleman, and she's afraid he might be homesick. It's his first time away from home."

Mr. Farrow smiled. "Has she had a letter from him? I'm sure I never thought to write when I was that age."

Eleanor smiled. "Not yet, but I expect he will send a few lines—he and Anne have been particularly close since Mama passed away."

Aunt Everley poured the tea and handed it around. "I'm sure if it weren't for Anne's affection for Henry he would have been sent to Mr. Smith earlier. Charles as well. It is hard enough for young ladies to take over the running of a house like Fairfield Hall without younger brothers in the way."

"Miss Travis was with us," Eleanor reminded her. "Sophie and I were still young enough for a governess, and she taught the boys too. I'm afraid most of the hard work of running the house fell to Anne, with Miss Travis so occupied with the other four of us."

"For the first few years," Aunt Everley agreed. "But you and Sophie have stepped up in the years since."

Eleanor wasn't sure she could quite agree to that. Sophie escaped outdoors with her Greek poetry more often than she strictly ought to, and Eleanor spent much more time practicing magic than a woman with a household to run should. But she couldn't correct her aunt in front of company without being rude, and to be fair, most of the spells she'd practiced were household spells to make things easier on Anne and the staff. <u>Most households made do without magic, unless a magician lived there, and Eleanor had had a beast of a time trying to find useful spells</u>. She'd designed several of her own and had accumulated a small library of spell books. But despite Eleanor's efforts to help, she knew Anne had shouldered most of the burden.

I never realized I said "beast of a time" here! How funny, because when Isabelle needs household spells in *The*

CHAPTER 3

Beast's Magician, she must have the beast himself invent or tweak them for her.

Anne joined them soon after, and Eleanor saw admiration in Mr. Farrow's face. She supposed that however good his income, a clergyman would prefer a hard-working, active wife to one of the young insipid beauties who'd never had to lift a finger unless it was to play the pianoforte. Anne sat on the couch beside Aunt Everley, with Mr. Farrow in a chair nearby. After some discussion of the weather and what Mr. Farrow had seen since coming to town, Mr. Weston was prevailed on by the whole group to tell them something of his sea battles. His assigned frigate, *HMS Reward*, had been in the fighting near Lissa and Toulon. He told only as much as could be acceptable for young ladies, particularly with their aunt present, but even so, the whole room was on the edge of their seats. The corner of his mouth quirked in amusement at their eager attention. Eleanor giggled and sat back. Sophie blushed and followed suit.

The *HMS Reward* is a ship I made up (not at all related to the ship of the same name built during WWII, which I didn't find out about until later), but Lissa and Toulon were sites of actual naval action during the Napoleonic War.

Chapter 4

Friday night held another card party. Eleanor contrived to sit as near the slightly open window as possible. She had no wish to feign another headache, nor to get a real one, and Aunt Everley kept a close watch on her for the first half of the evening. Seeing that Eleanor was settled in a good place, however, and that she showed no signs of indisposition, Aunt Everley turned her attention to the whist table. The card games were lively, and the only disappointment Eleanor felt in the evening was that Mr. Weston had not been among the party.

They spent the following evening at home, and Eleanor was perfectly happy to go upstairs with her sisters to prepare for bed early. Aunt Everley had assigned one of her maids to them, a widow of nine-and-twenty named Sarah, with auburn curls and a face full of freckles. She was cheerful and eager to please, but tonight they assured her that they were used to helping each other at home, and they could do just as well here.

"Getting ready in the morning is a different matter," Anne told her. "We'll want your help to dress for church. But we can handle preparing for bed on our own tonight."

So they were left alone. Eleanor locked the door, with both key and spell. Anne and Sophie had smuggled their own pale pink muslins into Eleanor's wardrobe earlier in the day, and now they changed into their evening dresses and matching shoes. Anne walked the perimeter of the room, Sophie muttered the spell at the wardrobe door, and the three of them slipped down the marble staircase to dance in the Faerie Queen's court.

The process was habit by now, having done it weekly for five years, but tonight it struck Eleanor how different their experience was to Mama's. <u>She never knew when memories of Mama would hit, only that they *would* come and that the frequency didn't diminish no matter how much time passed.</u> Now, as she walked through the marble tunnel with her sisters, Eleanor remembered Mama sitting on the edge of the bed where she lay snuggled with Anne, Sophie tucked in her trundle bed beside them.

"What story shall I tell tonight?" Mama's voice was smooth as satin and soft as silk.

"Faerie," Sophie begged eagerly.

Mama looked to Anne and Eleanor, and when neither of them protested, she began the story they'd heard more often than any other. "Once upon a time, when I was a girl of thirteen, I lay awake one night, unable to sleep. My sister Beatrice lay in the bed beside me, snoring, but it wasn't the noise that kept me awake. There was a strange kind of quiet in the house—a waiting, an expectation. Suddenly, I saw a man in my room, standing beside my window. I opened my mouth to scream but quickly stifled it. He was watching me, waiting to see what I'd do, so I watched him too. He was tall and elegant and flawless, and after a few minutes of staring at each other, he moved to the door to the nursery, which connected to ours. When he opened it, I didn't see the nursery. I saw a stairway lit by silver lanterns. He held out his hand to me, inviting me to come with him. Beatrice was still snoring, oblivious to my movement as I sat up and swung my legs out of bed. The man frowned at my nightdress, and suddenly I found myself wearing a ball gown, the kind that Beatrice wore now that she'd come out. I laughed and took his hand and went with him through the gate, positive that I was dreaming."

By this point in the story, Sophie's eyes had closed, her breathing slow and steady. Beside Eleanor, Anne gave a soft sigh and nestled deeper into her pillow. Mama lowered her voice and leaned in, telling the rest to Eleanor alone.

"He led me to a wide glade filled with the most beautiful dancers, and introduced me to the queen. I spent hours dancing with them. When the ball ended, he escorted me home, promising to teach me spells that I would need to come back. I fell into bed and slept soundly. When I woke in the morning, I was in my nightgown, and there was no sign of a magic land on the other side of the nursery door. I thought it had all been a dream."

"Until the next week," Eleanor breathed.

"Until the next week," Mama whispered back, nodding. She bent forward and kissed Eleanor's forehead. "Sweet dreams, my love, and don't be afraid to visit Faerie yourself if you get the chance."

Eleanor blinked away the memory as the Faerie Queen's colonnade opened out before them. She was grateful for each chance to visit Faerie, each night they got to experience the magic. It was a way she felt connected to their mother, as if she were living in one of Mama's bedtime stories.

Lord River greeted them as they approached, flanked by two familiar Fae gentlemen, Lord Storm and Lord Orion, and the three sisters joined the dance.

CHAPTER 4

Lords Storm and Orion make cameos in later stories.

They returned to Eleanor's room hours later, red-cheeked, bright-eyed, and breathless. This was how most of their excursions had gone when they were at home in Fairfield. They slipped away quietly, returned to their beds tired and happy, magically repaired their worn-out shoes, and no one ever noticed that they'd been gone.

James self-consciously smoothed his hands down the front of his coat and tugged at his cravat. Dressing the part of elegant gentleman in town had never been his favorite thing, and he was finding it harder to adapt after seven years at sea. The French didn't care if your cravat was pristine when their frigates started firing at you, and James had been too busy keeping up protective spells and designing his own magical attacks to give a fig about fashion.

Now, however, he stood in an antechamber in Carlton House, waiting for an audience with a member of the Regent's Council of Magicians, a friend of Lady Sterling's. His appearance mattered. Fortunately, though he'd forgotten most of his spells for daily life on land while he'd served aboard the *HMS Reward*, he'd found his old journals tucked away in a trunk when he'd returned. He hadn't read back through them all yet, but at least he'd found enough of the old spells to appear respectable.

Obviously, the Prince Regent was real, but the Council of Magicians was not. But it sounds good, doesn't it?

The antechamber was small and unexpectedly simple, given what James knew of the Regent's opulent taste. White walls, dark wood, gold damask. He paced the small area between the furniture, too restless to sit despite the ache in his leg. It was a shame spells for pain relief were so notoriously finicky. Most didn't work consistently, and the rest required some physical object to latch onto. And even the best of those that he'd found did nothing for the stiffness.

This will come back later.

The door opened, and a man blustered in. He was short

and wide, with receding white hair and an enormous silver mustache. His brown eyes were small and watery as he reached to shake James's hand.

"Weston, is it? Good to meet you, good to meet you," he said, gesturing to the chairs. "Let's sit and have a chat, shall we?"

"Thank you, Lord Wallace," James said, taking a seat across from him. "I appreciate you taking the time for me."

"Not at all, not at all. Glad to do it." The man waved a hand expansively. "You have quite a reputation, it seems. The *Reward* would have been lost several times over if it weren't for you, or so I've heard."

The back of James's neck heated, but he kept his eyes solidly fixed on Lord Wallace's. "We all did our part, my lord."

"Indeed."

Lord Wallace smiled so that his face crinkled like an old apple. James couldn't help liking him, despite his <u>resemblance to a well-dressed walrus</u>.

I kept wanting to call him Lord Walrus. It was somewhat intentional but mostly subconscious. He just appeared in my head exactly like that.

"So what can I do for you, son?" Wallace asked. "Seems to me you have the credentials to do whatever you like now that you're back on home soil."

"Well, that's just it." James frowned. "I'm at a bit of a loss. I was hoping you might have some ideas of where I might fit, where I might help the most. The majority of my recent spell work has been... specialized, to say the least."

Wallace chuckled and rubbed his chin. "You could say that, to be sure. I've heard that many military magicians set up in private practice when they leave the service. There may not be much of a need in a city the size of London, where we all seem to congregate, but Bristol, Portsmouth, Liverpool— there's clientele all over the kingdom waiting for a practicing magician to set up shop nearby, and more so in the ports if you've a knack for maritime magic."

James nodded. "I've considered that, but..." He shrugged. Somehow, magic-for-hire didn't strike the right chord with him.

This is one reason why he is such a good match for Eleanor. They both want their magic to matter.

"The pay's good," Wallace added. "You could also go into teaching at one of the universities, training up a new generation. I could write you a glowing recommendation. Military magic, nautical magic... You have more practical experience and expertise on both subjects than anyone in England since Lord Nelson."

It wasn't the worst suggestion, and James pressed his lips together as he considered it. He did have experience that most university professors lacked. But the idea of standing in front of a lecture hall of young men, blathering on about what spells to use in such-and-such wind conditions, was about as exciting as drowning in mud.

Lord Wallace didn't give him a chance to respond, however. He said, "You have an estate, haven't you? Didn't I hear Lady Sterling mention something about it?"

"I have," James said.

"Then why bother working at all, son? Go hunt and fish and relax in the country. You've earned a rest."

James shook his head. "With all due respect, my lord, I'm too accustomed to action to idly lounge about the country. I'd be bored out of my mind within weeks."

Wallace chuckled. "Can't say I blame you." He stood up and held out a hand. "Well, think about what I've said. I'll put in a good word for you wherever you like."

"Thank you." James rose and shook hands. Lord Wallace escorted him to the exit, where he bowed and took his leave. If asked, James couldn't have said that the meeting had been productive, as he hadn't been keen on any of Lord Wallace's suggestions. But he liked the older man, and it felt good to have another magician in his corner.

Early the next week, Eleanor and Sophie retreated to the sitting room after breakfast. Sophie sat down at the pianoforte.

"I suppose I had better learn this Italian song before the

party," she said, frowning at the foreign words on the page.

She began to play, and Eleanor moved to the table where she had left her spell book the day before. Eleanor still hadn't decided which spell she liked best. The rainbow spell was beautiful, but, as Aunt Everley complained, it made the room feel damp like fog for a while. Growing a violet was the one she'd practiced most, but violets were too small for an audience to see easily. She thought she might be able to make the violet grow larger than usual, but she wanted Lady Snow's help to get that part of the spell just right. That left the bouquet of roses.

Eleanor picked up the stick she'd been using, just a twig she'd broken off one of the trees in the park. She stared at the stick, concentrating on the spell-words with all the focus she could muster, as Sophie began the second verse of her song. A bud appeared at the end of the stick. Then several more. Slowly, the buds grew larger and pinker until they began opening. Soon Eleanor was holding a tiny bouquet of pale pink roses at the end of a twig. Sophie hit a wrong note, and the jarring chord broke Eleanor's focus. The roses vanished.

Eleanor sighed. Illusions required too much attention to make them perfect and hold them so others could see. Eleanor had been practicing this one for months, and she still couldn't manage more than a handful of roses at a time, and the smallest distraction made it all fall apart. Eleanor glared at the cup of water she'd used to practice the rainbow yesterday. She thought the spell-word, and the whole thing froze to a solid block of ice. She sighed and thought the reverse spell-word, thawing it again. At least some spells were easy.

Eleanor decided she needed a break, so she left the sitting room to see if Anne had finished her breakfast yet. She found her sister and aunt still at the table, but with the plates cleared away. Aunt Everley sealed a note and placed it with a pile of others on the tray for Harvey to take to the post. She pulled another sheet of paper closer and dipped her pen.

"Now," Aunt Everley said. "Who must we include in the invitations? We can fit ten couples at table."

Eleanor slid into the chair beside her sister. She was so frustrated with the rose spell that she was even willing to help make a guest list, which she hated. It involved too much calculation—Who had they dined with lately? Who would be offended if they were left out? How did they find enough single gentlemen to balance the fact that the Maybury family included three young ladies? It wasn't so bad at Fairfield, as their neighborhood was small, and they usually invited the same people.

"Colonel and Mrs. Hastings," Anne began. "We dined with them last week. And Lord and Lady York." She listed two more couples. "But that doesn't leave us with a very balanced table."

"No," Aunt Everley agreed, surveying the list she'd been making as Anne spoke. "All your choices have been correct. Now, what single gentlemen can we add? Lord Rupert is a good conversationalist."

"If we invite Lady Sterling, we can also invite Mr. Cole and Mr. Weston," Anne suggested.

"Excellent," Aunt Everley added their names to the list. "And that friend of Mr. Weston's... Mr..."

"Farrow," Eleanor offered. Her stomach was fluttering oddly at the thought of Mr. Weston and his friends joining them at dinner. Not because there was anything strange about dining together, but because they would be there in the evening to see the girls display their accomplishments. Eleanor had never done magic for a practicing magician before. Lady Snow didn't count; the Fae lady still saw her as a child, after all, and had been her only teacher since Mama passed.

"I've been having trouble with my rose spell," Eleanor ventured, as Aunt Everley pored over the list again. "I was thinking I might play instead."

Anne and Aunt Everley both looked up. Anne raised an eyebrow. "That's a worse fib than usual," she said. "You hate playing. You never practice."

Eleanor opened her mouth to argue, but Aunt Everley said, "Sophie is the best singer of the three of you. Your best accomplishment is magic, and everyone should see it. Choose a different spell to learn. You have two weeks."

"Do the violets," Anne said. "And don't worry. *All* of our guests will be impressed."

Eleanor excused herself and paced the hall for a few minutes before going back to the sitting room. Anne had always been able to read her too easily. Sophie looked up from the pianoforte when she entered and stopped playing.

"What's the matter?"

Eleanor sighed. *Both* of her sisters could read her easily. "Mr. Weston will receive an invitation to dinner."

"And you're afraid he won't come?"

"What? No!" Eleanor said. She blushed. "I'm afraid he *will* come. I'm not used to having such a knowing audience for my spells."

"Don't be ridiculous. I don't get worked up when I play for company, even when that company includes musically accomplished ladies."

"That just means you're braver than I am."

CHAPTER 4

Sophie laughed. "No, I just enjoy playing too much to let it bother me. And you enjoy magic too much. Read your book and find a new spell, or make one."

Eleanor shook her head, but she followed her sister's advice. Sophie went back to playing; Eleanor picked up her copy of *Ford's Magical Accomplishments for Young Ladies* and carried it to a chair by the window. She tucked her feet up on the chair beside her and opened the book at random, tracing her finger along her mother's notes in the margins. By the time Harvey appeared at the door to let them know that there were visitors in the drawing room, Eleanor felt calmer. She still didn't know exactly what spell she would do, but she always found peace rereading the spells that Mama had taught them. She also found a bit of courage from her own scribbled notes; she was good at magic, she understood it, and even in this new city lifestyle, that hadn't changed.

Chapter 5

Eleanor entered Lady York's drawing room on Saturday night with more trepidation than would be expected for a small, private ball. The furniture had all been removed to leave the floor open for dancing. The walls were papered in pale yellow flowers, and candlelight reflected off several mirrors. It was a pleasant room, and a pleasant-sized company—only ten couples could dance at a time. Unfortunately, the size of the party would make any absence more conspicuous, and Eleanor had already flatly refused to go home early with a headache.

Anne had learned from Aunt Everley that Lady York's house was not large enough for a full ballroom, so they ought not to expect a gathering such as they'd seen at Lady Sterling's. Anne had brought the news immediately to her sisters in a private conference. Sophie was all for one of them being "indisposed" again so that they could leave early, but Eleanor wouldn't hear of it.

"Lord River gave me an earful the night of my supposed headache," she said. "We need to find another way. He suggested opening the gate through a door there—at whatever house we are spending the evening."

Her sisters looked shocked at this idea, but as Eleanor remained unmoving, and as there were no better ideas to be had, they agreed.

Eleanor had spent the afternoon reading and rereading one of Mama's handwritten spells, practicing until she could do it perfectly and silently. It was one that she'd never had to use before, a spell to make one unnoticeable, so that if one was in the room—and hopefully if one left it—one would slip the mind and notice of any observers.

Eleanor's heart beat fast as she entered the ball with Aunt Everley and her sisters. They'd passed another open door in the hall: a saloon where card tables were set and refreshments laid out. Refreshments in another room would be a perfect excuse for leaving the drawing room. They paid their respects to the lady of the house, then mixed with the company, greeting acquaintance and being introduced to new people. Eleanor continued to marvel at how many new faces there always were in town, even after weeks of morning calls and evening parties, there were still more yet to meet. This evening they met the young Earl of Tarrock, a hazel-eyed, elegant sort of young man of perhaps three-and-twenty. He bowed gracefully and asked Anne for the first dance, honoring her as the elder sister, though giving Eleanor and Sophie admiring glances as well.

There was not space enough in the ballroom for everyone to be dancing, but Lady York knew how to throw a ball, and she had not invited so many guests that young ladies must sit out for long when they wished to be dancing. Eleanor only sat out two dances during the first half of the evening. She was already flushed from dancing when Mr. Weston asked her to favor him with the next, so she hoped that her blush went unnoticed. Try as she might to follow Sophie's advice and not worry about the magic she'd do at Aunt Everley's dinner party, she'd spent much of the week wondering what Mr. Weston would think of her magical display. Someone who had used his own magic to save a ship from sinking must be unimpressed by the little illusions and tricks of the ladies of the *ton*.

She accepted him readily, despite her embarrassment. His limp didn't decrease the agreeableness of dancing with him, and she had questions she wanted to ask.

"We haven't seen your friend Mr. Farrow in several days," Eleanor said. "Has he left town?"

"He has," Mr. Weston said. "He'll be back on Monday. He must be in church on Sundays and occasionally for other parish business, so he goes back and forth quite a bit."

"He must spend a lot of time on the road," Eleanor said, surprised.

"Fortunately, his parish is only a half day's ride from town."

Eleanor assented, then asked. "And you knew him first at Oxford?"

"He was one year ahead of me," Mr. Weston said. "He struggled with his magic lessons, and his Latin was infinitely superior to mine, so we traded assistance. I hadn't seen him since he left Oxford until you saw us renew our acquaintance in the park."

"Do you know anything of his family?"

"He's the third son of a baronet," Mr. Weston said. "He'll have no title, but I believe the living he was bequeathed is a good one."

The dance took them apart for several minutes, and when they came back together, Mr. Weston asked, "Is there a particular reason for your interest in my friend?"

"I thought he admired Anne," she admitted, glancing along the set at her elder sister.

"I believe he does," Mr. Weston acknowledged. "It would be

CHAPTER 5

hard not to admire her. All three of the Miss Mayburys stand out in the London crowd."

"Flattery again, sir?" Eleanor laughed.

"Truth," he said simply, but his mouth quirked at the corner.

He returned Eleanor to Aunt Everley in time for her to be asked for the next dance by the young Earl of Tarrock. During the dance, Anne and Sophie each made a point of giving her a significant look: this was the last set before they snuck away. Eleanor's heart began racing again, and she was barely aware of making halfway intelligent answers to Lord Tarrock's questions.

The dance ended; Eleanor joined her sisters. Anne made a comment about refreshments, and Aunt Everley nodded absently. On her other side, Lady York was sharing some apparently juicy gossip, and Aunt Everley was listening intently while trying to appear not to. This was the perfect opportunity. Eleanor took her sisters' hands and thought the spell-word that would allow them to leave the room unnoticed, then they wended their way around the room to the door. Once through, they walked down the hall, passing the saloon casually, arm in arm, as if they only needed a reprieve from the heat and noise of the dancing.

They stopped to try a door farther down the hall, but it was locked. Another across the hall opened, and the girls peeked inside. It was a library, and more importantly, there was a second door in the wall to the right. Eleanor nodded. Anne walked around the shelf-lined walls, and Sophie locked the door behind them. Eleanor went directly to the second door and thought the spell-word that would open the gate. The door opened, the lamplit marble staircase appeared before them as it always did, and the sisters slipped inside to their second ball of the evening.

James was standing by the drawing room windows, watching the dance and listening to George Cole list details about each of the ladies they saw. Town seemed to be overflowing with peers this Season, but that was nothing to the number of beautiful and accomplished young ladies trying to entice them into offering marriage. George was pointing out a pretty blue-eyed blonde—a Miss Sarah Young—who was heiress to twenty thousand pounds, when something tugged at James's attention. It was like a mosquito buzzing nearby, just annoying enough to be distracting. He tried to place the distraction—Was it someone talking loudly at the other end of the ballroom? Was one of the violins unexpectedly out of tune? But it wasn't a sound. A smell, perhaps? James frowned.

After a moment, the whatever-it-was got stronger. Now it was more like listening to a heavy rain falling outside. James glanced out the window. The night was clear, the moon half full. His senses were now extra alert, trained by years of study and even more at sea to be ready to respond. He began searching his mind for the spell-word he'd need next.

Magic. Of course. Someone was doing magic here.

Now that he knew what he was looking for, it was clear. There was a trace of magic in the drawing room, but most of it was elsewhere in the house. He looked around for the hostess. Lady York was talking animatedly to Lady Everley. A question tried to form in his mind as he looked at the second lady—something that he ought to remember, someone else he ought to look for—but it wouldn't come. He looked for the master of the house instead and didn't see him.

"Where's Lord York?" he muttered.

"Card room," George said, frowning. "You've not been listening, have you?"

"You were telling me about Miss Young," James said absently. He was scanning the room for any other known magicians. One of the mothers standing by the wall was frowning into the distance, but James suspected that that had more to do with a slighted daughter or a trodden toe than a sense of magic. No one else seemed to notice anything.

"Yes, I was," George said irritably. "Five minutes ago."

"Sorry," James said. How did no one sense such a powerful spell? And why was someone working it during a private ball? He had just opened his mouth to excuse himself when the spell stopped. Most of it, that is—the trace of magic lingered in the drawing room. James frowned around at the room, disoriented.

"Are you all right?" George asked.

"I'm fine," James said. "I just thought..." He stopped. There was no point in telling George about the magic.

After another moment, the trace of magic in the drawing room dissolved as if it had never been there. James continued to survey the room for any hints as to the source but without success. The song ended.

"I'm going to ask Miss Young," George said, shooting James a mystified glance and walking away.

James nodded, though his friend was no longer looking at him. It was taking some time for his wariness to fade. Seven years as the only magician on board the *HMS Reward* had made him extra sensitive to, and defensive against, any magic that wasn't his own, particularly if it came without warning or explanation.

When at length he'd calmed enough that he thought of dancing again, he looked around for Eleanor Maybury. She was already in the set. He sighed. He *was* supposed to be following Lady Sterling's advice not to dance twice with the same young lady. He began to make his way around the room, in search of a young lady in need of a partner.

He found Miss Sophie Maybury sitting out the dance. While she wasn't her charming sister, she was a bright, enthusiastic girl capable of carrying on an interesting conversation. He approached her and cleared his throat.

"Would you care to dance, Miss Maybury?"

Sophie looked up in surprise, and he noticed she cast her eyes around for her sister. His amusement grew as he realized she was looking for Anne, who was the usual Miss Maybury.

"Forgive me," he clarified. "I meant you, Miss Sophie."

"Oh, that's better." Sophie grinned. "I'm always Miss Sophie at home, whether Anne is around or not."

"I will do my best to remember. But would you care to dance?"

Sophie accepted, and they took their place in the set. After a few minutes, when the dance allowed, Sophie asked, "Do you read Greek, Mr. Weston?"

The corner of James's mouth quirked up. "I *can*, but I'd be lying if I said I *do*."

"Do you not like the epics, then?" Sophie asked. "I'd have thought you'd find *The Odyssey* interesting, or *Argonautica*, as you've spent time at sea."

"My adventures in the navy were nothing like Odysseus's voyage, I'm afraid. I saw not a single siren but a good deal too much of the French. And from them I would have died ten times over if I hadn't kept my eyes on what was before me and my head out of the clouds."

James glimpsed Sophie's scowl before they were separated for a moment by the dance. He felt a small twinge of guilt for implying that she had her head in the clouds, but it wasn't a wholly inaccurate insinuation. He couldn't stand the silly, misguided, all-too-commonly-held assumptions about life and warfare aboard a ship, and if her notions of maritime warfare were derived from Greek epics, he'd prefer to set her straight.

When the dance brought them back together, however, she seemed to have let her irritation go. She brought up a new subject.

"Do you like music?"

"I enjoy hearing it, but I confess my ignorance. I've never learned to read it or play it."

"Have you attended the concerts in Covent Garden?"

"Not yet this season, though Cole mentioned something about going next week."

James caught her poorly stifled sigh. She must like music a great deal and be disappointed in his inability to converse on the subject. This was why he hated to dance with strangers, and why he'd enjoyed the frank, outspoken company of the sailors and naval officers. Socializing felt like navigating a dangerous shoal, perils at every turn, never knowing when you'd run aground. He turned the conversation to the dance and the weather—uninteresting topics, but at least something they could discuss without him annoying his partner.

Any other introverts feel this truth with me?

Chapter 6

On Monday morning, Eleanor received a visit from Lord Tarrock. He bowed to her and Aunt Everley on entering the drawing room and handed Eleanor a bouquet of yellow tulips.

"I called yesterday, but the footman said you weren't accepting visitors," he said. "I would never have waited two whole days to call on you otherwise."

Eleanor blushed. "Our mother began a tradition of not allowing social calls on Sundays so that we could rest and enjoy time as a family," she said. "It seemed a good tradition to keep, particularly as the pace of life in town is so much busier than we're used to in the country, and the hours so much later."

A maid hurried forward with a vase, and Eleanor arranged the flowers and set it on the table beside her chair.

"Indeed," Lord Tarrock agreed, sitting in a chair near hers. "It always takes me a few days to adjust when I come to town. But at this time of year, there's nowhere I'd rather be. There's no sport in the country, and the weather's appalling."

"Do you hunt, then?" Eleanor asked.

"I do," Lord Tarrock said. "I ride one of the finest hunters in the kingdom, and I breed both hounds and terriers."

Eleanor could think of nothing to say next. She knew nothing of dogs, or of hunting, and had no interest in either.

Fortunately, Aunt Everley made a comment that Lord Tarrock's kennels must be quite fine. He confirmed that they were, and spoke for a few minutes about the care and breeding of dogs. Eleanor then expressed her ignorance about the types of dogs and what they were best at. Lord Tarrock launched into an explanation of how various animals were tracked and flushed out and which dog's size and skill was suited to each, and named a few of his hounds that had outshone even his own expectations. He seemed both flattered by her interest and delighted by her ignorance, enjoying the chance to instruct her on the finer points of hunting.

"Mansplaining" wasn't a term back then, but that's basically what he's doing.

He left after half an hour, and Eleanor sank back in her chair. She'd been polite and attentive, a model of interest and civility. It was an exhausting act, one that Anne had always done so much better.

"You did very well," Aunt Everley said quietly. "With practice, it will get easier."

"I don't remember visitors at Fairfield ever being so..." Eleanor waved her hand vaguely, unable to finish her sentence.

"No, I'm sure they weren't," her aunt said. "But your neighbors there—while straightforward and easy to talk to—were never titled or interested in marrying you."

CHAPTER 6

Eleanor sighed and looked at the vase of flowers on the table beside her. "The tulips are lovely," she said. "And it was a sweet gesture."

Aunt Everley nodded encouragingly. "I'm sure you'll find other subjects that you and he have in common when you see him again."

Eleanor wasn't sure what to expect of Almack's. The balls there were the pinnacle of the *beau monde*'s week, and what happened in that assembly could make or break one's social career. On the other hand, London balls could never hold a candle to dancing in Faerie. So she was neither impressed nor disappointed when she entered the ballroom for the first time with Aunt Everley and her sisters, nerves writhing in her belly. They greeted the patronesses, who supervised the entrants from a dais at the top of the room. Aunt Everley had introduced them to Lady Jersey and Lady Bathurst at previous events, and of the others, only Countess Lieven was at all intimidating.

Researching Almack's and the patronesses was fun, and I still probably have a file of research somewhere, but it really only shows up in a couple of scenes. A fact I found interesting: Almack's was named for its founder,

William Almack, whose name was originally William Macall (he just flip-flopped the syllables).

The room itself was large and open, with gilded columns and enough mirrors on the walls to make the room feel twice as large. What really caught the eye, however, were the people. The gentlemen wore dark coats and breeches and white cravats, their waistcoats being the only bit of color. The ladies all wore variations of white, whether muslin, silk, or crepe. But their headdresses and turbans, flowers, ribbons, feathers…. It was a strange kind of menagerie. Eleanor felt for a moment that she and her sisters were almost underdressed, coming as they did with only pastel ribbons and a few white flowers in their hair. She glanced at her sisters who stood beside her, surveying the room.

Sophie reached over and squeezed her hand. "You look more elegant than any of the ladies trying so hard to make an impression," Sophie murmured, lifting her chin as if daring the *ton* to think what they would.

They'd only been in town a little more than a month, so there were many new faces among the crowd, but there were a few Eleanor recognized, and she was soon asked to dance. She danced the first three sets, then returned to Aunt Everley and Sophie, who'd sat out the last set. A gentleman soon approached, in company with Lady Bathurst. She introduced him as the Marquess of Linfield, and they all made their bows. He smiled at Sophie and asked if she'd care to dance. Eleanor hid a grin. Aside from Sophie always wishing to dance, Aunt

Everley would faint stone cold if one of them were to turn down a marquess. Sophie accepted graciously and took the marquess' offered arm.

He was tallish and fair, not particularly handsome but not unpleasant to look at, and probably a few years past thirty. His smile seemed friendly, and Eleanor watched him lead Sophie to the dance.

Lord Tarrock soon claimed Eleanor's hand, and she couldn't help watching her sister and Lord Linfield. They were both smiling, seeming to enjoy their conversation, which was more than could be said for her. Her complaisant expression was becoming more and more forced as Lord Tarrock again monopolized the conversation with his own interests.

Once their partners had left them with Aunt Everley, Sophie pulled Eleanor aside.

"Dogs again?" she murmured.

"Horses."

Sophie grinned. "Poor Eleanor."

"You find it hilarious, don't you?" She wrinkled her nose at her sister. "Particularly because your partner was obviously more agreeable."

"He was. He enjoys music, and he wants to hear me sing. He... he said that I have a lovely speaking voice, so he imagines my singing voice would be heavenly."

Eleanor beamed. "Then he imagines correctly." She linked her arm through Sophie's. Hearing of her sister's success made it easier to shrug off her own frustration with Lord Tarrock, so that she was able to accept the next gentleman who requested a dance with a genuine smile.

At Anne's request, they stayed at home on Saturday night, ostensibly so that they would all be well rested for the dinner on Monday. On that understanding, the girls went to bed early, only to sneak through Eleanor's wardrobe door into Faerie.

Eleanor only danced a few dances before seeking out Lady Snow. They'd spoken at the last Seventh Night about Eleanor's spell for the dinner party, and Lady Snow had helped her find the right spell-word to make the violet grow beyond its usual size. Eleanor had been practicing all week, and she wanted to show the Faerie her progress. Lady Snow was dancing, so Eleanor accepted another dance with Lord Storm—one of the very few Fae that she recognized from one Seventh Night to the next—before approaching her friend and mentor when the dance ended. Lady Snow led the way out of the dancers, off to the side of the meadow where there was space to sit in the grass. Eleanor glanced uneasily over her shoulder at the surrounding woods: the Others lived among the trees, Fae creatures that were not as benign or elegant as those whom the Queen welcomed into her Court. Nothing could be seen in the shadows now, but Eleanor would have sworn that she'd seen luminous eyes peering at the revelers in weeks past—overlarge, golden eyes with black slits for pupils.

Spoiler: the Others don't play much of a role in any of

CHAPTER 6

the books, though they show up again in one later book and a companion novella (which you can find information on at the end of this book).

"Show me the spell you've been practicing," Lady Snow said, calling Eleanor's attention back.

Eleanor demonstrated the spell, and she was pleased both with her own progress and with the satisfaction on Lady Snow's face.

"Good," the Faerie said. "I think we can add some more—an extra touch that will make it dazzle."

Eleanor lost track of time as they discussed theory and spellwords. Lady Snow insisted that she try the new addition twice before going home to practice it on her own. Eleanor did, and was corrected, and did again.

"Eleanor, child."

Eleanor looked up, surprised, at Lord River standing before them. She hadn't noticed him coming, as the grass made for silent footsteps and the dance was still loud. Lord River held out a hand to her. She took it and stood up.

"It is the last dance before you and your sisters leave for the night. Will you dance with me?"

Thanking Lady Snow for her help, Eleanor went with him to the dance. He didn't say anything for the first few minutes, and Eleanor began to think they'd spend the whole dance in silence.

"You came here from a ball last sennight, did you not?" he asked finally.

"We did," she said, wondering what he would say about it.

"Did all go well when you returned?"

"Everything seemed to go very well," Eleanor said. "No one noticed that we had been gone, and no one commented that we were any more tired than usual."

He nodded once. "Well done."

They passed the rest of the dance in silence, Eleanor grateful to receive his rare praise. When the dance ended, she returned home with her sisters, elated as always but less breathless than usual, as she'd sat out half the evening with Lady Snow.

Eleanor spent the next day practicing Lady Snow's addition to the violet spell in the breakfast room. Sophie had taken over the drawing room to practice her own performance, while Anne sat with Papa and Aunt Everley in the sitting room.

Eleanor was the only one near enough to hear the commotion coming from the kitchen. She thought the final spellword, absently completing the combination as she got to her feet, dusting her hands over the bowl on the table before walking down the hall. She hadn't been in Aunt Everley's kitchen since coming to town. Anne had done the full tour of the house and had cast a few spells that they'd always used at Fairfield, but Eleanor hadn't been there since she was a small child visiting at Christmas and hoping to sneak gingerbread between meals. It was exactly as she remembered, a whitewashed brick room with wooden tables and cast-iron pots and pans hanging from hooks on the walls. The cast-iron stove took up a corner of the room, and the savory smells wafting from that corner made Eleanor eager for dinner. But her attention was drawn to the far side of the room, where a person she faintly remembered leaned heavily against a table, her graying head in her hands.

CHAPTER 6

Mrs. Hopkins had been Aunt Everley's cook for longer than Eleanor had been alive. <u>The woman was made of flint and steel, with arms like a blacksmith's and no patience for imperfection or indecision. Her kitchen was run with military precision, but she had a—tiny, imperceptible—soft spot for children</u>. Charles had discovered it, because he'd been the only one daring enough to brave her wrath, but once he'd shared the secret with his sisters, they'd each been slipped a treat and a wink more than once.

Eleanor struggled to reconcile her memories of the fierce cook with the aging woman taking slow and careful but slightly ragged breaths on the other side of the kitchen.

"Mrs. Hopkins?" Eleanor ventured. "Is something wrong?"

The cook's head jerked up, and she turned wide, panicked eyes on Eleanor.

"Miss Eleanor, is it?" The cook's voice held a glimmer of her old strength, and she tried on a polite smile. "Been so long since I've seen you. Can I get you a biscuit or a bit of cake?"

"No, thank you. I... I heard a commotion and wondered if I might help."

Running feet clamored in the door to the back garden, and a young man who couldn't be more than fourteen tumbled into the room. "Not a bit of ice to be had," he gasped, propping his hands on his knees. "Not for love or money, unless you want me to go to the magicians."

"No need for that," Eleanor said quickly. "I'm a magician. What can I help with?"

The boy looked unconvinced. Mrs. Hopkins frowned. "I shouldn't ought to tell you, miss, nor burden you with our problems, but I'll have to tell her ladyship anyway if I can't solve this. You see, we never received our delivery of ice on

Friday when it ought to have come, nor Saturday. If it weren't for her ladyship's dinner party tomorrow, I could have done without ice in the box for a day or two, but half the menu needs to be cold, and there's no time to plan a new one. Being it's the Lord's day, there's nobody delivering ice. I've sent Trevor here round to the neighbors, but they've none to spare. So I've either got to hire a magician or drive out to someone's country ice house and take a block for myself."

"There's no need for that," Eleanor said. "Your ice usually comes in blocks?"

"Yes, miss."

"Have you any bread pans not currently in use?"

The cook bustled to a cupboard and removed two rectangular pans. "What are you thinking to do with them, Miss Eleanor?"

"I'd like them filled with water, please."

Mrs. Hopkins poured water from a bucket into the two pans. Eleanor thought the freezing spell at each one. The cook and her young assistant gasped at the solid blocks.

Eleanor smiled. "We'll give those a minute to thaw around the edges and loosen from the pans before putting them in the icebox. I can make as many as you like."

The cook blinked at her, dumbfounded, then crushed her into a tight hug. Releasing her, Mrs. Hopkins pressed a hand to her heart. "Forgive me, Miss Eleanor. Forgot my place. But you just saved your aunt's dinner party and quite possibly my job. I thank you."

"I'm glad to do it." Eleanor sank into the one chair by the table. "Now, did you mention cake?"

Mrs. Hopkins chuckled and brought out the leftovers from the previous evening's tea. She cut a slice for Eleanor and set it before her. Before Eleanor began eating, she checked the pans of ice. They were already coated in a sheen of water due to the heat from the oven. Mrs. Hopkins laid the frozen blocks in the icebox, a solid wooden crate lined with sawdust and tin. Meanwhile, Trevor filled the pans from the bucket again.

Life is so much easier with indoor refrigeration, but it's convenient to have a magician in the house.

"Are you her only assistant?" Eleanor asked him.

"Today I am," he said proudly. "It being Sunday, she gave the rest of 'em the day off. Said I'd be a big enough help to her on my own."

Eleanor smiled and bit into her cake. The boy reminded her of her brothers, so eager to be grown up and trusted with adult responsibilities. Yet he still had that childlike wonder that lit up his eyes when she wordlessly froze the pans again.

They repeated the process four more times before Mrs. Hopkins declared the icebox at capacity and set to remain cold for some time.

"I'll come back and check in the morning," Eleanor assured her after thanking her for the cake. "I can make more ice if need be, or just add an extra freezing spell to what's there."

Despite filling up on cake, Eleanor felt lighter as she left the kitchen. Freezing spells were easy, familiar. And they were useful. Not like the finicky violet spell that was all for show with no practical purpose.

She sighed and settled to practicing in the breakfast room again.

Chapter 7

As Sarah helped her into her newest pale green silk gown an hour before guests were to arrive, Eleanor told herself she ought to feel confident. She could perform the whole series of spells for the violets, precisely and in perfect silence.

Instead, she felt slightly ill.

When she joined her sisters in Anne's room, Sophie took one look at her and said, "My, you're pale!"

Anne paused with her finger half twisted in Sophie's hair. "You really are," she agreed. "Are you well?"

Eleanor hesitated. Sophie shook her head.

"She's quite well," Sophie said. "It's nerves." She raised an eyebrow at Eleanor. "Stop worrying so much."

"You love magic," Anne said, turning back to Sophie's hair and whispering the spell-word to set the curl. She twisted another lock around her finger. "What's bothering you?"

"I've never performed for an audience." Eleanor's voice was faint, but at least it wasn't trembling.

"Of course you have. You show us all your new spells, and you've entertained after dinner before."

Eleanor frowned at her elder sister. "Family is different. And our neighbors at Fairfield are hardly London Society, however much we like them."

"We'll be watching tonight," Sophie pointed out. "And Papa and Aunt Everley. So you're still performing for family."

Eleanor sighed but decided not to argue. No matter what her sisters said, they wouldn't talk her stomach out of its knots. She went to the mirror instead and pinched her cheeks to try to bring out a little color.

When Anne had finished with Sophie's hair, she motioned for Eleanor to take the seat. She separated out the sections of hair in front that she would curl, then she braided and twisted and pinned the rest into a kind of elegant knot. She used the spell to keep the hair in place that she always used on Sophie's. Then she did the front curls. Eleanor looked in the mirror again.

"You're amazing," she told Anne. "I don't know how you do it."

"We each have our little specialties." Anne smiled.

Eleanor and Sophie worked together on Anne's hair. Sophie braided it and twisted it, not as elaborately as Anne had done Eleanor's but very elegantly. Eleanor twisted the curls in front. Then together, they went downstairs to join their father and aunt in the drawing room to welcome guests. Papa complimented them all on their appearance, and Aunt Everley pulled Anne aside to discuss again the expectations of the evening. It was Aunt Everley's dinner party, as it was her house, but she insisted on Anne taking part as hostess. As such, Anne wouldn't be performing, aside from briefly assisting Eleanor; she would be ensuring that everyone had tea and coffee and were comfortable.

Guests came. Eleanor was in conversation with Colonel and Mrs. Hastings and Lord Rupert when Lady Sterling and her son arrived, and behind them, Mr. Weston and Mr.

Farrow. For a moment she lost the flow of the conversation, coming back only when Mrs. Hastings leaned over to her and complimented her on Anne's behavior as hostess. Eleanor thanked her.

"Anne has been presiding over our parties at Fairfield for the last several years," she acknowledged, "but a party in town is so different, you know."

The rest of the conversation was unmemorable, and Eleanor was both relieved and nervous when dinner was announced and they all moved to the dining room. She hadn't been paying attention to Aunt Everley and Anne's careful seating charts, so she was surprised when she was seated between Mr. Cole and Mr. Farrow. She was sure that Anne had intentionally placed Mr. Weston farther down the table so that his nearness and conversation wouldn't make her even more nervous. Eleanor appreciated her sister's thoughtfulness, but she also found herself wishing to talk to Mr. Weston. Instead, she talked to his friends. She and Mr. Cole talked about the sunny weather they'd been having, and discussed their favorite places to walk in town. She and Mr. Farrow discussed books, finding that they had read many of the same. Dinner passed in pleasant conversation. Eleanor didn't notice what food was on her plate, or taste the bite or two of each course that she took out of obligation, for her stomach was not interested in food. But she did notice that Mr. Farrow's eyes and smile were often directed toward Anne across the table.

In the first draft, I gave Anne and Sophie each scenes

from their own viewpoints, particularly Anne because of her romance with Mr. Farrow. (Note similarities to Jane Bennet's subplot romance with Mr. Bingley? I can't remember if that was intentional.)

The ladies removed to the drawing room while the men remained over port and politics. Eleanor declined a cup of tea; she was afraid her hands would shake too much and she'd spill it all. Time went too slow and too fast, and Eleanor only heard one word in four of the ladies' conversation. She stood by the window and pretended to listen, smiling when the others laughed. The gentlemen joined them, and Anne and Aunt Everley were busy with serving tea and coffee.

Papa joined Eleanor at the window. He didn't speak, just looked out at the moonlit night. Eleanor took comfort in his presence. Papa had seen all her attempts at magic over the years, from the simple spells Mama had taught them as children to the more complex spells she'd learned from Lady Snow or worked out herself. He had always praised and encouraged her, never finding fault. She was sure that tonight would be the same, and she remembered Sophie's words in Anne's room: her family would be watching. No matter what anyone else thought, her family would be proud of her.

Once everyone had a cup of tea or coffee, Aunt Everley formally asked Eleanor if she would entertain them with a display of her magical accomplishments. A footman lit more candles around the room so that everyone could see. Eleanor felt all eyes on her as she went to the side table where she'd left

CHAPTER 7

her supplies. She took a handful of dirt from a bucket on the floor and a seed from a small paper packet. Standing so that everyone could see, she planted the seed in her palmful of dirt. Then she turned to Anne who had come to stand beside her.

Anne smiled and held her right hand out, hovering it several inches above Eleanor's. She sighed out the spell-word without moving her lips, so that only Eleanor was close enough to know it wasn't perfectly silent. A light drizzling rain came from Anne's hand, as if from a cloud, and soaked the dirt Eleanor was holding. The water that didn't land on the dirt evaporated into the air as if it had never been. Anne breathed the second spell-word and the rain stopped. Then she gave Eleanor a quick, encouraging smile and sat down beside Aunt Everley.

Eleanor focused her mind on the wet dirt and on the seed underneath it. She thought the first spell-word, and the seed began to sprout. A little seedling poked out of the soil. Eleanor watched it grow and develop, waiting for just the right moment before thinking the next spell-word. The bud and its stem grew bigger and bigger before opening out into a violet three times the normal size. Eleanor heard a few murmurs from the audience, but she ignored them. Now was the time for Lady Snow's final trick. She closed her eyes and her fist, concentrating hard on the spell-word she'd worked out with her Faerie mentor two nights before. Eleanor knew before opening her eyes that it had worked perfectly. She blinked down at her fist. She opened it and shook the dirt—dry, flowerless—back into the bucket. Then she turned her back on everyone, to take a rag from the table and wipe the dirt from her hands. A collective gasp went up, and Eleanor felt a smile tug at the corners of her mouth. The window's dark reflection showed her profile, including the side of the elaborate knot of braids Anne had created. Surrounding the knot, tucked into the braids as if they had grown there—which, in a way, they had—were a cluster of violets.

I've loved this spell since the moment I started writing it.

Sophie began the applause, getting up from her seat on the sofa with Lady York and coming to hug Eleanor. "See?" she whispered in Eleanor's ear. "Nothing to worry about. You were perfect."

Sophie let go and went to the pianoforte. She began with a concerto, allowing time for the gathering to murmur amongst themselves before she started to sing.

James watched Eleanor cross the room to stand beside Lady Sterling's chair. Without thinking, he moved to follow, arriving just in time to hear Lady Sterling say, "That was quite impressive. Simple but elegant. Don't you think, James?"

<u>Eleanor looked around at him in apparent surprise and—was that alarm? Did she not want to see him? Had she been avoiding him intentionally all evening?</u>

Lady Sterling was waiting for his response, however.

"Very impressive," James agreed. Eleanor's shy smile encouraged him. "May I, Miss Eleanor?" He gestured to her head.

She turned away so that he could see the violets. The light purple of the flowers contrasted nicely with her dark hair. The temptation to touch one to see if it was real or an illusion was so strong that James had to clasp his hands behind his back. As she turned back around, he saw the petals shiver from the movement: real petals, real flowers.

Eleanor looked up at him, her silver-gray eyes holding his, a blush blooming across her cheeks. "Remarkable," he said quietly. "And in silence, too. Who taught you?"

"Our mother taught us when we were young," she said. "An… old friend of hers took over my magic instruction after Mama passed away."

"What spell books did they teach you from?"

Lady Sterling cleared her throat. James glanced at her, startled. In his eagerness, he'd forgotten she was there. Lady Sterling looked pointedly at the pianoforte.

"Shall we step back and allow Lady Sterling to enjoy the performance?" He moved around behind her chair into the open space in the corner. Eleanor followed. "I'm sure to hear about my rudeness later. Your sister's playing is excellent, but I can't pass up this opportunity."

He meant opportunity to talk about magic, but he was just as glad for the chance to stand close to her. He smelled wildflowers—Her perfume? The violets?—and between that and her silvery gaze, he was thankful that it was her turn to come up with what to say next.

"As my sister mentioned once before, I'm always happy to talk about magic," Eleanor said. "Mama taught us from *Ford's*.

Most of the spells I used tonight were adapted from there."

"That final trick can't have been from *Ford's*," James said. "I've never read the book, but that doesn't seem to be a common ladies' accomplishment."

Eleanor hesitated, blushing. "The last bit was from Mama's friend. She uses… unconventional spells, and she often creates her own." She watched him closely as she said this.

It was always safer to use tested and tried spells from reputably published spell books, but James was no stickler. He had often composed a spell on the fly while at sea, and he saw no reason why a lady of talent shouldn't do the same.

"Please give her my compliments," he said. "And my highest compliments to you as well—I have not seen a display of magic since I've been back in England to equal what you did tonight."

At that moment, Sophie began to sing in Italian. Eleanor's attention was drawn to her sister at the pianoforte, and James listened cheerfully to the performance, his eyes drawn to Eleanor as often as to Sophie, thinking that this had been the pleasantest dinner party of the Season.

Eleanor applauded with the rest when Sophie finished singing. She gave Mr. Weston a smile before moving toward Anne. The display of accomplishments was over; now conversation would reign until carriages were called. Aunt Everley presided over the tea and coffee if anyone needed a refill. Anne had been a spectacular hostess, but Eleanor felt that she ought to see if her sister needed any help. It was the excuse she gave herself, but if she were being honest, she'd admit that as much as she enjoyed talking with Mr. Weston, she was still nervous and shy in his company. His response to her performance was encouraging, to be sure, but would he still be so interested if he knew the larger spells she could do? Or if he knew that she wrote her own? He had shown no dismay at the idea of a lady designing her own spells, but did that only apply to older, established ladies who taught magic?

She was nearly to Anne when she saw Mr. Farrow address her sister, so she redirected her steps to accept a cup of tea from Aunt Everley, which she carried to the window. Looking out at the darkened street, Eleanor could hear most of Anne's conversation with Mr. Farrow. She silently chided her reflection in the dark glass for eavesdropping, but that wasn't enough to get her to move away. It was a crowded room, after all, and it couldn't be considered a private conversation if half the company could overhear.

"Have you heard from your brother yet? The one you were writing to a fortnight ago?" Mr. Farrow asked.

"I heard from Henry but two days ago. The shortest letter I've ever received, but probably the longest he's ever written to anyone." Anne laughed. "It was half a page, only one side of the paper. When I wrote to him, I used a full sheet, both sides, and I had to stop myself from writing over it cross-wise, because I was sure he wouldn't be able to make it out."

During the Regency era, there were no envelopes as we

know them. The letter's paper was folded, generally leaving the outside blank for privacy. But paper was expensive, so to use their space efficiently, people would write on both sides, leaving a little space for the address. If they still needed more space, they'd turn the page 90 degrees and write "cross-wise" over what they'd already written.

Mr. Farrow laughed too. "That sounds exactly like a sister and brother. Is he well?"

"Quite. He wrote that he likes Mr. Smith, and Mr. Smith's horses and dogs, and that Charles is teaching him how to shoot."

"Just like a younger brother indeed," Mr. Farrow chuckled. "I'd like to hear more about your brothers. Your sister said you and Henry became very close after—I'm so sorry—after your mother passed."

Eleanor held her breath. She had been the one to mention that fact.

"Yes," Anne said. "He was only six years old, and he had nightmares for several months. I stayed up with him when he couldn't sleep, and we spent a good deal of time in the kitchen drinking warm milk." She paused, and Eleanor could imagine her grimace. "I've never much liked it, but it seemed to do him good."

Eleanor risked a glance at the couple. Mr. Farrow's blue eyes were bright and interested, his manner inviting. Eleanor wondered how much more Anne would say. She rarely talked about the time after Mama's passing, even within the family. To her delighted surprise, Anne rewarded Mr. Farrow's gentle curiosity. Eleanor strained to hear Anne's soft murmur.

"I was sixteen then, and Mama's death was so sudden—she gave birth early to our baby sister, and then they were both gone in less than two days—it was a shock, of course, and… completely overwhelming. I was suddenly the lady of the house, with only half an idea of how to run things and <u>a little brother who clung to me like a shadow all day and kept me up half the night. But Henry needed me</u>, and for those first few months, caring for him was the only thing I felt like I knew how to do." She sighed, and Eleanor's heart ached for her sister. They'd all been young and dealing with their own grief, but she wished she'd been more support to Anne. "After a while he started following Charles around instead, chasing each other outside, romping with the dogs, learning to ride—in short, being a little boy."

"How old was your brother Charles?"

"Ten. He was too old to need his sisters, so he spent most of his time in the stables, attempting to shirk his lessons, then Papa sent him to be educated with Mr. Smith."

Eleanor heard the brief pause when Anne's vulnerability became uncomfortable. She knew even before she heard the forced lightness in her sister's voice. "But that's all history now. Tell me about your parish. I have never been to Essex, but Aunt Everley speaks fondly of her time there."

Mr. Farrow gamely spoke of his parsonage and his father's nearby estate. His was a family living, bestowed on him because he was the only son who'd gone into the church. Eleanor, having little interest in country parishes, allowed her mind to wander. Her gaze found Mr. Weston across the room. He was talking with Mr. Cole and Lord Rupert, but <u>she had the strangest fluttery sensation that he'd been looking at her only a moment before.</u> She blushed and returned her empty cup to the tea table, allowing herself to be drawn into conversation with Lady Sterling and Mrs. Hastings.

Chapter 8

Cole showed up at James's lodgings the next morning. James had been up for hours, having still not adjusted to the *ton*'s habit of sleeping until noon. He set aside the old journal he was reading and ushered his friend in. His rented lodgings consisted of two rooms, one for sleeping and the other for dining and entertaining company. They were both tidy with minimal furnishings, everything ship-shape and in its proper place. Cole took the seat across from the one James had just vacated.

"Tea?" James asked. "I was about to have some myself."

"Please."

The kettle was already full, and James thought a spell-word at it. It instantly began to boil, and he poured the water over the tea leaves in the ceramic pot. As he set it on a tray and carried it over, Cole chuckled.

"You say you've forgotten magic for daily use, but I can't see it."

"Sailors like coffee," James pointed out. There had been plenty of opportunities for him to boil water in the last seven years.

"Is that the only spell you've used this morning?" Cole raised a skeptical brow. "Did you tie your cravat by hand?"

James shook his head, his mouth twitching. "If I had, it would have been a perfect nautical knot, because those are the only knots I can tie."

"My point stands."

James chose not to argue. Cole knew how out of place he'd felt on returning to England. He'd missed the sea and the motion of the ship; he'd missed the crew that had become something like family in their time together. But more than that, he'd felt disconnected to his magic, suddenly finding the naval spells he'd used for years unnecessary, and being unable to recall so many of the spell-words he'd known before. It was as if he'd temporarily lost his identity. Reading through his old journals had slowly given him back that connection. With each spell he read in his own untidy scribble, he remembered three more. It had taken months, but he was finally feeling like a true magician again.

"What brings you by, aside from complimenting my cravat?"

Cole chuckled. "I was thinking of going out to Tattersall's today and thought you might join me."

James shrugged. "I don't see why not." He wasn't in the market for a horse at the moment, but he wouldn't mind a change of scenery for the day.

Cole nodded and drank half his tea in one swig. "What did you think of Miss Eleanor's violets last night? It was all a bit too small to make much of a show—hard to see from across the room." He eyed James for a reaction.

Warmth flooded James as he remembered standing close to Eleanor, watching the purple petals dance in her dark hair, smelling the wildflower scent of her. He ignored Cole's critique of her performance. "She's incredible," he said.

"Everything you ever dreamed of in a wife?" Cole smirked.

"I wouldn't know. I never gave it much thought."

This wasn't strictly true. Ever since meeting Eleanor, he'd found himself considering more and more what life could be like with her in it.

He'd had no intention of marrying before he turned thirty, planning instead to devote the first decade of his majority to adventure and the service of king and country. He'd never thought much about what he'd want in a wife when the time came. But peace had arrived sooner than he'd looked for it, and so had Eleanor. Even now, however, he was reluctant to marry until he knew what he wanted to do with his life.

James realized that Cole was watching him, waiting for more. "She's..." There were so many things he could say. Sweet, intelligent, beautiful, gifted. He suspected that she'd understand and empathize if he ever told her about the disconnection he'd felt. Magic seemed as central to her life as it was to his. "She's everything I never knew I wanted," he said finally. But now that he'd met her, he couldn't imagine settling for anything less.

"I suppose you'd better start courting her in earnest, then," Cole said. "Tomorrow. Today is all about horses."

James drained the rest of his tea and got to his feet, more motivated to get through the day.

On the sisters being alone together in the sitting room Tuesday morning, Eleanor complimented Anne on the dinner party.

"You always host well," she said, "but to host well in London takes something more."

"Aunt Everley will expect you to host the next one," Anne said. "She'll say you need practice before you marry."

"No, she won't," Sophie argued. "You're the eldest, and she's old-fashioned enough to focus all her attention on getting you married before she worries about Eleanor."

"Sophie's right," Eleanor said. She kept her eyes on her needlework. "And speaking of marriage, what do you think of Mr. Farrow?"

She glanced sidelong at her sister and was rewarded with a blush. Anne's response was perfectly composed, however.

"I think he's sensible, intelligent, agreeable—"

"Good looking," Sophie ticked items off on her fingers, "with a good living—"

"Sophie!" her sisters protested.

Sophie spread her hands in a delicate shrug. "It's true."

"It is, but that's not what's important," Anne said. "Not to me." She frowned at her knitting for a long moment, then said quietly, "All I want are a comfortable home, a pleasant companion, and something useful to keep me busy."

Eleanor tried to hide a grin. "I think Mr. Farrow would be quite happy to provide you with that." Anne shot her a look, and Eleanor gave up hiding her smile. "He spoke to you for longer than was strictly polite when you had duties to your other guests."

"Mr. *Weston* was eager to speak to *you* last night too," Sophie said to Eleanor. Anne favored her with a grateful smile for changing the subject. "Enough so that neither of you heard a note of the concerto."

"That's why you played the concerto," Eleanor pointed out.

CHAPTER 8

"We both listened to you sing."

"And his eyes were turned more often to you than to me."

Eleanor blushed. She hadn't noticed that. She'd been enjoying Sophie's song and trying to ignore the fluttery feeling in her stomach at standing so close to Mr. Weston.

"Did he compliment you on your performance?" Anne asked. Eleanor nodded.

"Well, he ought to, she was brilliant," Sophie said. "I did say she was worried for nothing. And I think he may have hit on the thing Eleanor wants above all, even more than Anne's 'comfortable home'—being recognized for her magical ability."

"Not quite." Anne frowned. "Eleanor's always been known for being gifted. Anyone acquainted with our family recognizes her skill." She looked thoughtfully at Eleanor. "What *do* you want most?"

Eleanor studied her embroidery for a moment. She had barely taken two stitches during the whole conversation. "I like your picture of happiness," she said. "But I want more. I want to do something useful with my magic, more than just the little daily spells to run a home and look after children. I want to make someone's life better, make a lot of people's lives better." She thought of the ice for Mrs. Hopkins, and the violets of the night before. Growing the violets had been a tricky series of spells, but it hadn't made a difference in any way.

Sophie seemed to know what she was thinking. "You never did like the performance spells. It's a shame the bigger ones don't make much of a show. I wonder what Mr. Weston would say if he could see you do *those*."

"He might actually smile," Anne said with a smile of her own. "He came close last night."

Sophie laughed, and even Eleanor let out a giggle. Mr. Weston's serious expression had been greatly softened by his eagerness and enthusiasm as they spoke of magic, but he hadn't quite broken a smile. Eleanor wondered what it would look like if he did, and if she could ever be the reason for it.

After talking with her sisters, Eleanor couldn't stop thinking about what she'd told them, about wanting to make a difference with her magic. It was absolute truth, and she'd been trying in small ways to improve life for her family and neighbors. But what was holding her back from doing more? There weren't many options available to lady magicians, and fewer to young, unmarried ladies of the *ton*, but Eleanor determined to ponder the problem from every direction until she came to some concrete ideas.

On Wednesday, Eleanor returned from business in Bond Street with her aunt and sisters to find that Mr. Weston had called and left his name. She sighed her disappointment at missing him but pretended it didn't bother her—her sisters already teased her about their apparent mutual interest, no need to make it worse.

That evening they attended Almack's again. Eleanor enjoyed the dancing, but she felt that everyone at Almack's was pretending to be something they weren't, putting on a show for the benefit of the *ton*. She danced with Lord Tarrock, who fortunately felt that he'd educated her enough on the breeding

CHAPTER 8

of hunting dogs and horses. He spoke of hunts he'd been on and wagers that he'd won. It was a shame, Eleanor thought, as their dances ended. He was a gallant gentleman, and she wanted to like him, but he was so full of his own interests that he hadn't yet shown an interest in her.

Anne and Sophie seemed to enjoy their evening. Though Mr. Farrow wasn't there, Anne didn't sit out a single dance. Sophie danced with the Marquess of Linfield again. He was a connoisseur of music, and he mentioned again that he'd like to hear her play. Sophie told Eleanor all of this as they sipped lukewarm, weak lemonade and wished for the cold, clear water of the Seventh Night balls.

Lord Linfield was quite serious in his desire to hear Sophie play. He called the next morning, and in the course of his visit, requested that she might sit down to the instrument. She obliged—she never required much encouragement to play the pianoforte. Eleanor watched a soft smile overspread his face as he listened. He never took his eyes from Sophie. He listened more intently than she'd ever seen anyone listen to music, except perhaps Sophie herself.

They received several gentleman callers most mornings. After this visit, the Marquess became a frequent visitor, and he often asked Sophie to play. Mr. Farrow, Mr. Weston, and Lord Tarrock also called often. It seemed to Eleanor that not a morning passed without one or more of them sitting with them in the drawing room or asking them to walk out. Once or twice, Eleanor sensed some awkwardness, even jealousy, as Mr. Weston and Lord Tarrock arrived at the same time, but both were too well bred to do more than send each other dark looks. Not all their visitors were so genteel; one of Anne's callers said something rude to Mr. Farrow about being a third son, and Aunt Everley had Harvey escort him from the house.

"I will not have you being impolite to my other guests," she told him firmly. "If you wish to court my niece, you must be civilized."

Anne blushed and apologized to Mr. Farrow, who shrugged and smiled and ignored the slight. But Eleanor, watching them in the absence of her own suitors, thought he was less animated for the rest of his visit.

Chapter 9

Despite using all her free time to plan ways to help people, Eleanor lacked plausible, workable ideas. She finally brought it up at breakfast, hoping Papa and Aunt Everley could guide her.

"Do you know of any good charities nearby?" she asked.

"Why?"

Aunt Everley ignored Sophie's blunt question and responded to Eleanor. "Kittering's Home is only a few blocks away. I give them an annual sum—not as much as I could give when your uncle was alive, but the work they do is important."

Aunt Everley's voice grew a little thick. Eleanor knew that not being able to have children had long been a sore point for her aunt. Supporting a home for orphaned children must be a way to assuage that pain, though she wondered why her aunt and uncle had never adopted any.

"Why do you ask, Eleanor?" Papa smiled, always supportive.

"I thought I might volunteer." She shrugged, trying to downplay how important this was to her. "I doubt they have a magician on staff or money to hire one, and I might have spells that could help."

"That's a brilliant idea," Anne agreed. "Are you going today? I'll come with you."

Sophie already had plans with a friend she'd met at Almack's, so she begged off, but she promised to join them next time.

After breakfast, Sarah met them at the door as they donned bonnets and gloves. "Her ladyship asked Mrs. Hopkins to send this along." She lifted the large hamper of food in her hands. With a bemused smile, she added, "And Mrs. Hopkins begged me to thank you, Miss Eleanor, for the ice."

Eleanor grinned. "I'm at her service any time."

The three of them headed out, opting to walk to the orphanage because the weather was so fine. Eleanor was still adjusting to the idea of needing a chaperone or a maid whenever they went out, as country rules of propriety were entirely different. But Sarah was cheerful and obliging and seemed just as happy to be going out as they were.

Kittering's Home sat in a long row of brick houses. They'd left the fine houses of the *beau monde* a block or two back; these homes were smaller and plainer but still well kept. Eleanor wondered how a house this size could shelter more than a handful of orphans, even if they were packed as tightly as sardines. She observed the outside of the building as Anne stepped up to the door and knocked. A young girl opened it, gawping at them with wide eyes.

"We've brought a donation of food," Anne said, giving the girl a kind smile. "May we bring it to the kitchen?"

The girl nodded, stepping back to let them inside and leading them back along a short hall to a dim, cramped kitchen with one small, open window. A girl Eleanor's age was peeling potatoes at a table. She smiled at them and set down the paring knife. The younger girl who had answered the door disappeared back down the hallway.

"I'm Lissy. How can I help you?" She wiped her hands on

CHAPTER 9

her apron.

"We've brought a donation," Anne repeated, gesturing to the basket in Sarah's hands.

Lissy moved the bowl of potatoes to the seat of a chair, and she and Sarah unpacked the hamper. The girl's eyes went wide as she took in the assortment of fruit, vegetables, cheese, butter, and fresh-baked bread.

"Thank you." Her voice rang with sincere gratitude. "Everyone will be so excited, the little ones especially. There's only so much I can do with potatoes and bread, and they get tired of such a limited diet."

"Do you do all the cooking?" Eleanor asked in surprise.

Lissy nodded. "I have helpers. I was Old Miss Bea's assistant for years—I've lived here since before I could talk—so when she died, the kitchen passed to me." She smiled and shrugged. "It's a good life. I have a home, food to eat, and a family to share it all with. I need no more."

"I see that," Eleanor said. She wasn't sure she could have said the same as her eyes roamed the small room. She'd want a bit more sunlight, for one thing. Her gaze fell on a pair of buckets by the door to the back alley. An idea occurred to her. "Where do you get your water from?"

"There's a pump in the middle of the square," Lissy said.

"And those are the buckets you use?"

The girl nodded, confused. Eleanor cast one of the spells she'd designed, speaking the spell-word aloud for Lissy and Sarah's benefit. "Now when you draw water, the buckets will clean it before you use it. The magic doesn't work instantly, I'm afraid; the water needs to sit in it for about a quarter hour. But then it's as pure and fresh as if it came from a mountain stream."

Lissy's mouth fell open, and she stared at Eleanor. "You're a magician?"

Eleanor nodded.

"But why…?"

"If your water is dirty, you're more likely to get sick," Anne explained. "Clean water tastes better, and it will help everyone here stay healthier. We have the spell on all of our water jugs at home."

Unsanitary conditions were one of my biggest roadblocks in writing a Regency book. I just couldn't put my poor characters through all that. So I gave them magic to help.

"But why help us?"

"Why not?" Eleanor said. "You're just as worthy of help as anyone else, and I'm able and willing to give it. In fact, we have the whole morning free and a handful of other useful spells."

Lissy gaped at them, dumbfounded, then said, "I'll take you to Mother Kittering."

Eleanor and Anne exchanged glances. From behind them, Sarah said, "I'll stay and peel potatoes for her, if you don't mind, Miss Maybury. I'll do my part to help too."

"Thank you, Sarah," Anne said before following Lissy out of the kitchen.

Lissy led them back to the front of the building, then into

what would normally be the drawing room. It was set up as a kind of schoolroom, with mismatched desks aligned to face the fireplace, where a petite middle-aged woman stood by the mantle, correcting the six young children who were reciting the alphabet together. The woman looked up when they entered, brushing a wisp of mousy brown hair behind one ear.

"Keep practicing together," she instructed the children. "I'll be just a moment."

She crossed the bare wooden floor and greeted them with a curtsy. "How may I help you?"

"Mother Kittering, these ladies are magicians wanting to volunteer," Lissy said. "Said they had spells that might be useful."

The middle-aged proprietress looked taken aback, but she rebounded quickly. "We're grateful for aid of any kind, aren't we, Lissy? What did you have in mind?"

Eleanor's mind went to the spell she and her sisters used to repair their shoes at the end of each Seventh Night. "If you have any mending that needs done, I have a spell for that. And if any of your children have an aptitude for magic, I can teach it to them."

"We also have a spell that makes windows repel dirt so they don't need to be washed as often," Anne added.

Mother Kittering clapped her hands together. "You're a pair of blessed angels," she beamed. One of the little boys at the desks had stopped practicing his alphabet and was watching them. Mother Kittering waved him over. "Connor, go find Robert and Celeste. Have them come to the back parlor, please. And then I'd like you to take Miss…" She looked at Anne.

"Maybury," Anne supplied.

"Take Miss Maybury around the house and show her all the windows."

If little Connor thought his instructions unusual, he didn't say a word. He darted from the room, hollering as his feet thundered up the stairs for the two children he'd been sent to find.

"If you'll wait here," Mother Kittering said to Anne, "I'll just take your sister into the back parlor where we keep our mending."

Eleanor grinned at Anne before following tiny Mother Kittering through a door on the far side of the schoolroom. She realized, as she entered a nearly identical room on the other side, that Kittering's Home actually occupied two of the homes in the row, connected by a door that had been cut into the dividing wall. As the proprietress led her to the stairs, Eleanor could see through another door that the back room opposite the kitchen in the other half of the house was occupied by a long dining table with benches on either side. There must have been a door between kitchen and dining room that she hadn't noticed.

The room above was set up as a small parlor. A threadbare sofa and two wooden chairs with embroidered cushions made up the furniture, positioned to receive light from the lone window on one side and from the currently unlit fireplace on the other. Beside the chair nearest the window sat an overflowing basket of clothing, a sewing basket perched precariously on top. As Eleanor entered, a boy and girl of about ten skidded into the room behind her.

"You wanted us, Mother Kittering?"

Both children had flaming red hair and bright green eyes. They were slight, healthy but underfed. Their skin and clothes looked clean, however, and they eyed Eleanor with open curiosity.

"We've been blessed with a visit from a magician," Mother Kittering said. "She'll teach you a mending spell so that we needn't do it all by hand."

The boy, Robert, couldn't hide his dismay at the domestic task, but Celeste's expression lit up. "No more sewing?" The hope in her voice made Eleanor bite her lip to contain her grin.

"Not as much mending," Mother Kittering corrected. "It's still a skill to learn and practice."

Celeste sighed. "Yes, Mother Kittering."

The older woman bustled out, and the children turned their attention to Eleanor. "I understand you both have an aptitude for magic?" she said.

Robert nodded. "Our papa was a magician, or so Mama said before she died and left us here." His matter-of-fact tone didn't fit with the heartbreaking reality of what they must have lived.

Eleanor took a deep breath to loosen the tightness that clutched at her chest. "I'm sorry," she said. "My mother died too. My name is Eleanor."

"I'm Robert, and Celeste is my twin," he said. "You're really going to teach us magic?"

"I have one spell for you today. If I think of any more that could help you, I'll come back and teach it to you another time. For now, however…"

Eleanor moved the sewing kit off the top of the basket and lifted off the top garment. It was a pair of trousers with holes in the knees. She spoke the spell-word aloud, slowly and precisely, and enjoyed the gasp as the children saw the tears mend.

"Can you repeat the word after me?" She spoke the spell-word again, and they echoed her. "Good. Now, as you say it this time, I want you to look down at your own clothes and concentrate on them being whole and new."

They did as she asked. It took a few tries, but both succeeded. The elbows of Celeste's blouse, which were nearly worn through, lost their translucent threadbare quality. The patches from the knees of Robert's trousers fluttered to the floor as the original fabric repaired itself, releasing the stitched-on additions. They grinned at each other and then at Eleanor, and she laughed.

"It's more fun this way, isn't it?"

Celeste nodded. "Much more fun than pricking myself with a needle all day."

"I don't think I'd mind doing girl chores if I could do 'em with magic," Robert admitted.

"That's good," Eleanor said, "because we have a whole basket to get through."

Together, they worked their way through the basket, item by item. Eleanor made sure that each garment was folded and stacked neatly on the sofa once it had been repaired. At last, they reached the final pair of socks in need of darning. Eleanor fixed those, and then they piled the clothing back into the basket. Robert and Celeste each took a handle of the basket to go put the clothing away.

"When you're done, go see Lissy in the kitchen. Magic requires food and rest, and you've both earned an extra snack for all your work today."

Their eyes grew wider than ever at the promise of extra food. Eleanor made a mental note as she parted ways with her helpers to ask Mrs. Hopkins to send over another hamper.

CHAPTER 9

She returned downstairs to the schoolroom and found Anne sitting in a chair, reading a picture book to the handful of young children who had abandoned their desks and sat close around her feet. Eleanor hadn't realized how long the mending had taken. The Home had so few windows that Anne must have been finished long before. She wasn't surprised that her sister had found a way to interact with the youngest orphans, nor that one of the littlest girls had crawled into Anne's lap. Anne had always been good with children.

When the story was done, Anne closed the book, carefully placed the little girl back on her own two feet, and rose. "I'll come again another day," she promised the children, who pleaded for more stories.

Eleanor and Anne gathered Sarah from the kitchen, said goodbye to Mother Kittering, and began the walk home. Anne was smiling brighter than she had since Henry had gone to school. Eleanor couldn't stop thinking about Robert and Celeste and the other kids she'd met. She knew they'd done a good thing today, and she had no doubt that she and Anne would come back and volunteer again, but it didn't feel like enough. Doing a little only made her want to do more.

This visit to the orphanage was not in the first draft. I'm really glad I added it later, because I love these kids. Other scenes that didn't exist in the first draft were James's meeting with Lord Wallace (Walrus) and his visit to Tattersall's with George Cole.

James was on his way home from Lady Sterling's house when he saw Eleanor and her sister walking. His heart picked up speed, and he hailed them, barely taking time to check for oncoming carriages before jogging across the street to them. The way Eleanor's face lit up when she saw him caused him to trip over his own feet. If asked, he'd blame it on his knee. It had been feeling somewhat better now that the rain had let up, but he'd never admit to the real cause of the stumble.

He forced himself to look at Miss Maybury as he bowed. If he kept looking at Eleanor, he'd forget to speak. "Where are you ladies off to today? May I escort you anywhere?"

"We've just come from Kittering's Home," Miss Maybury said, naming an orphanage down the street. "You're welcome to walk us home."

He'd been hoping for such an invitation. Offering an arm to each sister, he asked what they'd been doing at the orphanage. They told him about magically cleaned windows and mended clothes and about reading to the children. He listened intently, admiring the sisters more and more.

"It was all Eleanor's idea," Miss Maybury said.

Eleanor blushed, and James felt another piece of his heart fall at her feet. "I just want to use magic to help people," she said, meeting his eyes for the first time since he'd joined them.

"I know just what you mean." His own desire to do something useful with magic was exactly why he was having so much trouble settling on a new vocation.

CHAPTER 9

Eleanor tilted her head. He could practically see ideas taking shape in her mind. "I wonder if you might be willing to help me with something," she said at last.

"Anything I can do, I'm at your service."

She explained another spell she'd used at the orphanage, a spell to clean drinking water. "It takes a quarter hour for the full effect, but even in a minute or two there's a noticeable difference."

"Fascinating." He hadn't been able to tear his eyes from her face since she started talking. "I'm assuming this wasn't from *Ford's*."

"No."

"Another from your mother's friend, I suppose? But why do you need my help with it?"

Eleanor skipped over the first question and addressed the second. "The spell works well in private homes, and I've done what I could for the families in our neighborhood. But if it were used on vessels in workhouses and hospitals and the homes of the poor—how much unnecessary illness and suffering could be prevented?" She glanced away, as if embarrassed by her earnestness, though he found it charming. "I have only so much influence, but you—as a gentleman, a well-respected magician, and a naval hero—could do so much more. I hoped you might use some of your influence to put the spell where it could be of service."

They stopped walking. James suddenly realized that they'd reached Lady Everley's house while Eleanor had held his full attention. He'd entirely forgotten that Miss Maybury and the maidservant were with them as well.

Miss Maybury said a quiet farewell and went inside. The maidservant hovered at the foot of the steps, waiting.

James allowed his gaze to return to Eleanor's. "I'm honored that you've asked this of me," he said. "If you'll write out the spell, I'll do my best to be worthy of the charge."

Eleanor's brilliant smile melted him. She shuffled through her reticule before pulling out a scrap of paper and a pencil. At his slightly raised eyebrow, she said, "I never know when I'll want to jot down an idea for a new spell. And sometimes weeks pass before I can talk to Mama's friend about it."

James felt a smile tugging at the corner of his mouth. She was one of a kind. "You're wonderfully prepared."

She held out the scrap of paper with her neat, curling script forming a single spell-word. He took it, looked it over, then folded it and tucked it into his waistcoat pocket.

Unable to think of a good excuse for lingering, he said, "It's been a pleasure seeing you, Miss Eleanor, as always."

"Likewise," she said, her silvery eyes sparkling. "And thank you."

Chapter 10

Anne was waiting for Eleanor inside. "Why didn't you tell him you wrote that spell?"

Eleanor took her time tugging off her gloves. "I'm still not wholly certain what he thinks of me," she said slowly. "He's only seen me doing illusions; perhaps he's looking for a lady with only the typical magical accomplishments."

Anne shook her head. "He wouldn't have been so interested in our volunteer work today if that were the case." She laid her bonnet and gloves on the table by the door. "Anyone can see that he admires you. I hardly think having too much magic is going to frighten him off."

Eleanor silently conceded her sister's point. A magician who'd served in the war was unlikely to be intimidated by a young lady, regardless of her ability. But her affinity for magic felt like a very personal detail, one that she didn't broadcast. It was tied too closely to Faerie and Mama, Lord River and Lady Snow. By now the *ton* had seen that she had skill with illusions, but only her family knew of the spells she designed herself, and only her sisters knew about Faerie.

"Do you think he'll use the spell?" Anne asked.

"I hope so." For the sake of the poor of London, she hoped so, but also for herself. She wanted Mr. Weston to win his way into her confidence, and getting her spell into the right places would be a giant step in that direction.

The next morning, Mr. Farrow and Lord Linfield called within a few minutes of each other, and as it was such a fine day, they all decided to walk out. The party divided into groups: Anne and Mr. Farrow walking together, and Sophie and Lord Linfield together, with Eleanor making a third. Eleanor paid the flowers more attention than she ever did, and she took it upon herself to be the one greeting and conversing with any acquaintances they passed. Even so, she couldn't completely ignore the conversation between her companions.

"Do you enjoy reading, my lord?" Sophie asked.

"I read the newspaper every morning," he replied, "and the almanac when it comes out. I recently read a book with an interesting take on crop rotation. I sent it along to the steward of my Yorkshire estate—we'll give the ideas a trial there before deciding if it's worth implementing on my other estates."

Sophie nodded, but said nothing.

Eleanor could tell her sister was disappointed—Sophie wanted everyone to read Greek epics with as much fervor as she did. To give Sophie a minute to collect herself, Eleanor said, "Do you take a great deal of interest, then, in the running of your estates?"

"I do," the marquess said. "I feel I would be remiss in my duty if I did not. Just last week my steward came to town, and we discussed ways to improve the drainage of one of the lower fields—it floods with any heavy rain."

Eleanor nodded politely, and she saw Sophie putting in extra effort to appear interested, as Lord Linfield continued to discuss crops and drainage and yields and cold storage. At last he fell silent.

With dismay, Eleanor noticed that they'd only come a third of the way along their usual path. Never had time seemed to go so slowly. She went back to looking at the flowers, and, to save Sophie from a renewal of the conversation, took the opportunity to exclaim, "Look at those violets!"

Sophie eagerly exclaimed over them as well, though violets weren't her favorite flower. The open stretch of grass was so littered with tiny flowers that the whole field was purple.

This happens in my backyard every summer, and I love it. Violets aren't my favorite flower, but I love seeing a field of purple.

This led to a discussion of flowers in general. Lord Linfield gave few opinions on the subject, though he admitted that he'd always liked apple blossoms.

The rest of the walk passed in light talk on subjects Eleanor and Sophie introduced. That evening, Eleanor slipped into Sophie's room when they went upstairs to dress for dinner. Eleanor helped Sophie out of her walking dress.

"So, this morning…" Eleanor began, holding the new dress for Sophie to wriggle into.

Sophie let out a long sigh as she put her arms through the sleeves and arranged the dress. "He doesn't even read novels."

"But he likes music."

"He does," Sophie nodded. "He also likes talking about crop rotation." She made a face.

Eleanor laughed. "He probably has multiple interests, and maybe another of them won't be so…"

"Boring?"

Eleanor grinned. "It felt like the longest walk I have ever been on."

Sophie groaned and fell back onto her bed. "And I was so hopeful! He listens to me play with such appreciation!"

"Give him a chance," Eleanor said. "He likes music, and he likes you. That shows good judgment. And if he cares about how his estates are run, well, that's a good thing too, isn't it?"

"I suppose," Sophie sighed. "I'm glad you were with me for that."

"Anything for my sister," Eleanor said with a grin. She left Sophie to finish getting ready while she went to get dressed herself.

Saturday evening found them all at another ball, hosted by the Duke of Harrington and his lady. The ballroom was large, brightly lit with chandeliers, and full of elegant people. Eleanor

CHAPTER 10

had never seen so many titled peers gathered together in her life, not even at Almack's. She half expected the Prince Regent to arrive at any moment. As such, she was surprised to see that Mr. Weston had been invited—she knew he was from a good family, and he was a cousin of Lady Sterling, but he had no title himself. But as she and her sisters followed Aunt Everley and Papa through the crowd, greeting acquaintances and, as always, making new ones, she noted an astonishing number of military gentlemen: admirals, colonels, captains.

Before she could ask, Papa explained, "The Duke of Harrington is a great friend to both the army and the navy. He served in the army himself, and his younger sons have both been in the service as well. He's giving this ball in honor of his friend, Admiral Hart, who was a great hero in the war and who will soon be married."

So Mr. Weston's position as a magician in the navy gained him entrance. Eleanor was glad to see him, and glad that the title of magician was considered on a level with the other military ranks. But she thought he looked less than comfortable as they passed him in the crowd.

Eleanor didn't see much of Mr. Weston once the dancing started. By now she had a large acquaintance, and she didn't lack for partners. Lord Tarrock had just asked her for the next dance and was leading her onto the floor for a waltz when she saw Mr. Weston coming toward them. He stopped as he saw her with another gentleman, his expression darkening as he noticed who her partner was. She didn't doubt that he had been hoping to have this dance himself. She smiled at him, despite his frown, hoping he'd ask her later.

In real life, jealousy sucks. In books? Love it. That's literally Lord Tarrock's whole purpose in this book—to give James a little competition. Tarrock obviously doesn't stand a chance at winning Eleanor's heart.

Lord Tarrock had noticed Mr. Weston as well, and he frowned as he took Eleanor's hand in his, placing his other at her waist. "I seem to see that Weston fellow everywhere. How has he made such a place for himself in society? He has no title."

"He's a cousin of Lady Sterling," Eleanor said. She didn't point out that Mr. Weston was young and handsome, because no gentleman liked to hear that about another, though it certainly affected how one was received by the *ton*. "He's also something of a war hero."

Lord Tarrock snorted. "I hardly think doing parlor tricks in the middle of a battle makes a man a hero."

Eleanor was saved from responding by the beginning of the dance. Every retort she could come up with was unpardonably rude. She was offended on Mr. Weston's behalf, but she was also stung by Lord Tarrock's dismissive attitude toward magic. She didn't know if he had any idea that she could do magic, let alone how passionate she was about it. In all of his visits, he had never once asked.

Mr. Weston was nowhere to be seen by the time the waltz ended. Eleanor danced twice more before her sisters found her. She thought the spell-word that would make them unnoticeable, and together they slipped out of the ballroom to find an unoccupied room in the duke's mansion with an extra door through which they could open the gate.

James stopped, stock still in the middle of the crowd at the edge of the ballroom. There it was again, that mosquito-buzz of magic. He didn't know enough of the other guests to know if any were magical, either to be casting the spell or noticing it. Nobody else appeared to observe anything unusual. He forced his way politely toward the door. Before he escaped the crowd, a stronger sense of magic began, just as it had at the Yorks' ball. It was a non-auditory rush, like a downpour of rain, noticeable in a noisy ballroom because it wasn't strictly a sound that one could hear. He made it into the hall, and he followed the magic along a side corridor to a closed door. He tried the handle; it was locked. He thought the spell-word that would unlock most ordinary bolts, and he heard it click, but still the door wouldn't open. He tried several other spell-words to no avail. He probed at the spell blocking the door, but he couldn't find out enough about it to break through. James stepped back to lean against the wall across the hall, frowning at the door. It wouldn't do to be caught trying to break into a door in the duke's residence. But he couldn't let the magic go uninvestigated. He'd already been trying for several minutes, and if this spell was anything like the one he'd witnessed at

Lord York's, it would end in a few minutes more. He retreated to the end of the corridor where it met the main hall and leaned casually against the wall to wait, as if he'd just needed some breathing room. From here he'd be able to see the spell worker leave the room.

"Weston, there you are!"

James jerked upright in surprise. Colonel Hastings strode over to him, beaming.

"I see you've escaped the dancing," the colonel said. "Come, join us at cards. I'd like you to meet a friend of mine—I told you about him at Lady Everley's dinner, remember—he's just in here."

Colonel Hastings put his broad hand on James's shoulder and steered him down the hall to the card room before James could come up with a good excuse for remaining where he was, or even any reply at all. The colonel introduced him to a Captain Franklin, and they talked for a few minutes before James managed to excuse himself, claiming he'd promised a lady a dance. Rather than going to the ballroom, however, he hurried back down the side corridor. It was too late: the door was open, the magic was over.

James returned to the ballroom, figuring he ought to dance so that what he'd told the gentlemen wasn't a complete lie. He was preoccupied and distracted, however, and hadn't made it far into the room before he ran headlong into a young lady. He caught her arm to keep her from falling and was halfway through a hurried apology before he realized who it was. Eleanor Maybury looked startled, but her silver eyes sparkled as if she was about ready to laugh.

James couldn't miss this chance. "Dance with me?" he blurted.

Heat rushed to his face. If he'd had a single spell that could take him anywhere but there, he'd have been gone in an instant. To look a fool in front of her, of all people… Could he have asked her in a less gentleman-like way?

That adorable giggle. "Yes, of course," she said. He offered his arm, and she took it, as if this hadn't been embarrassing or awkward in the slightest.

They joined the dance. James was distracted in whole new ways now because Eleanor was smiling at him. But even that couldn't take his mind completely off of the magic he'd sensed. It struck him abruptly that Eleanor was a magician. Why hadn't he thought to look for her before, to see if she could sense it too? He didn't know if she could sense when other people did magic, he'd never had an opportunity to ask, and he wasn't sure how to bring it up now.

"Did you…" He hesitated. "Did you notice anything unusual earlier this evening?"

Eleanor frowned, confused. "Nothing," she said. Then a smile played at the edges of her mouth. "Unless you refer to your being a moment too late to ask me to waltz, though I can't imagine that's particularly unusual in such an assembly."

James's mouth quirked as he suppressed a smile. "No, I don't imagine it is," he agreed. "But I shan't let it happen again. I'll take this opportunity to ask: will you do me the honor of saving the first waltz for me, whenever we next happen to be in the same ballroom?"

Eleanor grinned. "I would be delighted."

They went down the dance, and when they were near enough to talk, James tried again, not that he was upset about the previous digression. "Have you often been around other people practicing magic?"

"Not often," she said. "Only my mother and my sisters; rarely another young lady performing in company."

"Can you tell when a spell is being performed if you're not in the same room?" he asked.

"I don't know," she said, her smile fading and a furrow forming on her brow. "My sisters and I always practiced together. Why do you ask?"

James decided not to alarm her. He didn't know what she would think of spell work being done in a duke's mansion during a ball, but he'd heard of ladies with catastrophic imaginations, and he would rather see her smile. "Curiosity," he said mildly. "I've had so few opportunities to speak about magic with young ladies, and I've never met one with your skill."

"Can *you*?" she asked. "I mean, can you sense when a spell is being done somewhere else?"

"Sometimes," he said. This wasn't strictly true—he could nearly always sense something. "It depends on the distance and what else there is to distract me. Naval training, you know."

"Would you have known I was growing violets at Aunt Everley's party if you'd still been in the dining room?"

"No, not in such detail," he said. "I would have known that someone was doing magic, and probably what level of difficulty the spell was, but that is all."

"Then it's a good thing you were in the room to see it," she said lightly, with a teasing grin.

"It is indeed."

Chapter 11

Eleanor cornered her sisters after breakfast the next morning. They slept late every Sunday, given the extra hours of dancing they squeezed into each Seventh Night, so Papa and Aunt Everley were done and in the sitting room or library before the sisters came downstairs. Eleanor dismissed the servants and leaned toward her sisters.

"I think Mr. Weston sensed our magic last night."

Anne paled.

"What do you mean?" Sophie gasped.

"He asked me if I'd noticed anything 'unusual,'" Eleanor said, "and then he started asking whether I can tell when other people are working magic, even if it's in a different room." She frowned at her untouched eggs. "He said he was only asking out of curiosity, but I think it was more than that."

"Did you ask him what he can sense?" Anne asked.

Eleanor nodded. "He can sense the magic itself—not what the spell does, but the complexity."

"So he couldn't tell that the magic was ours," Anne said.

"Or that we'd opened a gate," Sophie added.

Eleanor nodded again. "But maybe we should go only if we can leave from my room, at least for a few weeks."

Her sisters instantly protested. Sophie was loud enough in

her argument that Eleanor shushed her and glared a warning. Sophie subsided, but scowled and stabbed at her eggs with unnecessary force. Eleanor was sure that Anne would come to agree with her—her elder sister was steady and intelligent and generally quite reasonable—but she knew she'd be facing more whispered arguments with Sophie before the next Saturday night.

Tuesday morning dawned gloriously sunny, and when Mr. Farrow and the Marquess of Linfield called at nearly the same time, a walk was proposed again. They fell into the same divisions as they had the previous week. Eleanor could tell that Anne appreciated having a tête-à-tête walk with Mr. Farrow, and she knew Sophie was grateful for her help finding conversational topics with Lord Linfield.

Fortunately, Sophie almost immediately brought up music, and Eleanor was able to listen with only half an ear while her sister and the marquess discussed the favorite subject. She was still somewhat preoccupied by worry over what Mr. Weston had sensed at the ball, but she was also distracted by watching Anne and Mr. Farrow who walked a few yards ahead.

Mr. Farrow's usual ease and cheer had been replaced this morning by awkwardness and silence. Eleanor could see by the set of his shoulders that he was uncomfortable, and from the quick twitches of Anne's head, she guessed that her sister was shooting glances at him, waiting and wondering what to say.

Eventually, the two began talking, and Eleanor suspected that the subject was serious, but she couldn't overhear a word from where she was. Sophie soon called her attention back, and Eleanor spent the rest of the walk trying to introduce new subjects as Lord Linfield somehow managed to turn every topic back to politics.

Eleanor had never been so relieved to return home. The gentlemen remained for a few minutes, and Eleanor noticed that Mr. Farrow's demeanor had lightened significantly. When they'd left, Aunt Everley went to see the housekeeper about dinner.

Anne turned to Eleanor and Sophie, who had both collapsed back into their chairs.

"How did you enjoy the walk?"

"Lovely day," Eleanor managed.

Sophie nodded as if she were fighting with herself. Suddenly she blurted, "Politics!"

Eleanor giggled weakly.

Anne looked from one to the other, confused.

"That's all Lord Linfield talked about," Eleanor explained. "There must be a big debate in Parliament going on. Lord Linfield could speak of nothing but taxes, tariffs, and imports, no matter how we tried to turn the subject."

"And exports," Sophie reminded her. "And fines, and more taxes." She pressed a hand over her eyes. "Last week it was all agriculture."

"Was it really?" Anne asked, eyes laughing. "You never told me."

"It was," Eleanor confirmed with a grimace.

"You said that he probably had other interests," Sophie

accused.

"I did, and I was right," Eleanor agreed, a smirk replacing the grimace. "Unfortunately, his other interests aren't any better."

"Oh, poor Sophie," Anne said sympathetically. "He seemed so pleasant when he spoke of music."

"That's the only subject we share an interest in," Sophie said. "And even I can't talk about music forever. I think I'd die of boredom if I had to spend a whole day in his company."

Eleanor exchanged looks with Anne. The expression was dramatic and not strictly polite, but they didn't doubt its truth.

"But what about you, Anne?" Eleanor asked, leaving Sophie to her sulk. "You seemed to enjoy the walk." She hoped Anne would share whatever had been going on between her and her beau without Eleanor needing to pry.

"I did," Anne said with a small smile.

"Did he propose?" Sophie lifted her hand slightly from her eyes.

"Not yet." Anne blushed. "But he hinted that he would. He admires me, and he said he's looking for a wife who is good with children."

"Which you are," Eleanor said. "And it's been obvious from the start that he admired you." She frowned. "But why is it so important that you're good with children?"

Anne's blush deepened. "Because he has a two-year-old daughter at home."

Eleanor blinked. "I didn't know he had been married."

"He hasn't."

Eleanor stared at her sister. Even Sophie lowered her hand and sat up. It was no secret that many men sowed wild oats when they were young, nor that unfortunate—even abandoned—children were often the result. But Mr.

Farrow? Eleanor supposed it was a mark of honor and honesty that he had acknowledged the child and was telling Anne up front, but her whole perception of the clergyman was shifting uncomfortably.

Anne's eyes widened as she realized what her sisters were thinking. "No! Oh heavens, no, not that. He adopted her after her parents died."

In the first draft, when Anne still had scenes from her POV, she was the one who misunderstood and was appalled.

Eleanor sagged slightly in relief.

"Her father, Mr. Farrow's best friend from childhood, was killed in battle abroad. Her mother died in childbirth months later. Neither had any living family, so Mr. Farrow adopted the child and has been raising her with the help of his mother."

"What's her name?" Eleanor asked.

"Andrea," Anne said. "She was named for her parents—her father was a Captain Andrew Gorse, so her full name is Andrea Mary Gorse Farrow." She smiled. "It's too long a name, but he wanted her to have something of her parents."

Sophie bit her lower lip. "That's the sweetest thing I've heard in months."

"Isn't it?" Anne said. "He wants me to meet her. He's almost too good. I'm waiting to find a fault."

Eleanor grinned and jumped to her feet. She bounded over and wrapped her arms around Anne's shoulders. "I'm so happy for you!"

"Why?" Anne asked, beaming.

"Do I even need to say?" Eleanor asked. "Because he's perfect for you, and he clearly thinks you're perfect for him too."

Footsteps in the hall sent Eleanor back to her seat, and they spoke of other things as Aunt Everley rejoined them. But Eleanor caught Anne smiling more throughout the rest of the day than an evening at home could warrant.

James opened his door and surveyed the man waiting in the hall. He was tallish, probably just shy of forty, with curling light brown hair. His brown eyes were half hidden behind thick spectacles that looked in danger of sliding off his nose.

"Mr. Weston?" The man smiled and held out a hand. "Dr. David Miller. Thank you for agreeing to see me."

"Your note intrigued me," James said, stepping back to give his guest room to pass. "Please, come in. You heard of me from Lord Wallace?"

"I did." Miller took the offered chair and declined tea. "He's my uncle. When he told me of your injury and how you used magic to ward off infection and sepsis, I couldn't rest until I spoke with you." He pushed his glasses back up the bridge of his nose. "I apologize for the impertinent and personal nature of the inquiry, but I'm a surgeon, and magic and medicine blend so rarely."

James nodded. "Ask me whatever you like, and I'll answer as best I can."

"Will you start by telling me exactly what happened, from the wound to the spells and healing? My uncle's account was third- or fourth-hand and lacked specificity."

James sat back in his chair and did his best to give details without letting the memories of that day overwhelm him. He'd been holding several protective spells plus a binding spell on the hull of the ship to hold it together despite the shattering effect of enemy cannon. The pistol shot to his knee had knocked him from his feet, but adrenaline had kept him from feeling the pain or the magical drain until after the battle had been won. Another British ship, *HMS Julep*, had come alongside the *Reward*, having sustained less damage. *Julep*'s magician had taken over the binding spell on the hull, allowing James to let go of all the spells he was holding. He'd passed out, coming to hours later as the ship's cook was cleaning the wound. James had demanded food, washing down stale bread with burnt coffee, fueling himself for more magic.

The first spell he'd used had been a magical tourniquet. He'd designed that spell himself soon after joining the navy, and he'd used it with many shipmates' injuries over the years. The ball had fractured the top half of his kneecap and lodged just beside his femur. He used the same binding spell on the bone that he'd used on the ship, holding it together in one piece until it healed. After the cook had dug into the wound to remove the ball and before sewing it shut, James had used another spell to clean it. The spell hadn't been intended for flesh, and it burned like hellfire, but he didn't doubt that it had worked.

He'd spent the next two weeks on bed rest, eating and sleeping as much as possible while he maintained the binding spell on his knee. Every few hours he repeated an altered version of the cleaning spell to avoid infection.

This is another scene that wasn't in the first draft. I enjoyed writing the account of James's injury and figuring out what magic he'd use to deal with it.

"Astonishing," Miller said, sitting forward in his chair, elbows on knees, fingers steepled together. "I believe you did more medical magic in those first days than anyone has in generations."

James, slightly disoriented from the memories, didn't know what to say. He simply watched the doctor and waited.

"I've been interested in merging magic and medicine for years," Miller went on, pushing his glasses up again. "My family has produced several skilled magicians, yet the most healing they've ever done was to lower a fever. And I'm sure I don't need to tell you about the limitations of magical pain relief."

James gave a wry grimace. "No. I'm very familiar with that subject."

Miller chuckled sympathetically. "But you, Weston, give me hope. If you and I worked together, I believe we could revolutionize healing. There's been far too little collaboration between the two disciplines, in my opinion. Each side is focused on their own concerns without considering the good—the necessary—that the other brings to the table. What do you think?"

James considered the doctor for a long moment. "I think you make an excellent point," he said at length, "and I agree that magic could be doing more. I need some time to think more on it, but I'd like to talk again."

"Splendid!" Miller, beaming, jumped to his feet and heartily shook James's hand. "We can do a great deal of good together, you and I. I look forward to it."

On Thursday morning, Mr. Weston called while Mrs. Graham and her daughter were sitting with them. Aunt Everley was fully engrossed in conversation with Mrs. Graham. Anne and Sophie drew all of Miss Graham's attention, discussing some new sheet music Miss Graham had found in Bond Street and what songs they preferred above all others.

Eleanor had been hoping for just such a moment. She had chosen a seat by the table rather than close by the couch where her aunt sat. She caught Mr. Weston's eye and inclined her head toward a chair near her. He readily took the invitation. As he seated himself, Eleanor debated whether she could ask more about what he'd sensed at the ball the other night, but she decided against it. She didn't know how to ask without giving away that she'd been involved, and she'd rather not know how much he suspected.

"I'm afraid I haven't had the opportunity to try your spell yet," Mr. Weston murmured. "I've been in and out of meetings for what seems the past month."

Eleanor hid her disappointment with a smile. "I understand you're busy," she said. "Would it be too bold to inquire about the meetings? I imagine they're nothing like the teas and visits that I endure."

Mr. Weston gave a soft huff that was almost a chuckle. "Some, I'm sure, are more interesting. I met with a surgeon just the other day with some intriguing ideas. But 'endure' is a good word for others. Yesterday I spent all morning in discussions with the admiralty and other naval magicians seeking to improve training."

"What changes are they hoping to make?"

"Everyone has different opinions," Mr. Weston said, "which is why they've needed so many meetings. The best idea so far is to recruit sailors as magicians, men who joined the navy as boys and are accustomed to life at sea. Magicians who come to the job after years of schooling have a much harder time adjusting."

"You did well enough," Eleanor pointed out.

"I was one of the lucky few who took to it right away," he agreed.

His attention was soon called away by a question from Mrs. Graham. Eleanor suppressed her resentment as they joined the conversation with the others. She always wished for more time to speak with Mr. Weston alone. The world of practicing magicians was fascinating. *Mr. Weston* was fascinating. <u>She was sure that if they were given hours to themselves, they could fill it with conversation and she'd still wish for more time.</u>

CHAPTER 11

After visiting for an hour, their guests departed. Eleanor rose with Aunt Everley to see them out. Mr. Weston bowed over her hand, giving her a look that felt both intense and significant, though Eleanor couldn't quite decide why.

Aunt Everley's smile suggested that she'd seen the look and had interpreted it, and that it boded well for Eleanor's chances. Eleanor blushed, glad when her aunt excused herself to write a letter in the parlor.

Returning to the drawing room, she paused with her hand on the door when she heard her sisters' voices. She ought to stop eavesdropping, but Sophie's words froze her where she stood.

"It's not Mr. Weston," Sophie was saying defensively. "Really it isn't. He doesn't care about music, and he doesn't like the books I like, and, I promise, I stopped thinking of him as a possibility after the first week."

"But…"

"But he's like one of the old epic heroes," Sophie said wistfully. "He's been to sea, and he's fought in battles, and he'd face down the world for Eleanor. That's what I want. Not *him*, but *that*."

Eleanor's stomach twisted at the thought of her sister's jealousy. Her heart ached for Sophie, but it also raced at the idea of Mr. Weston caring that much for her. *Would* he face down the world? Could she be that important to him already?

"What about Lord Linfield?" Anne asked. "I know he's a good deal older than you, but—"

"His age isn't the problem," Sophie said. "He hasn't got a heroic bone in his body. Or even a romantic one."

"I doubt you'll find many men that have."

"Mr. Weston has. And Mr. Farrow has, adopting his friend's

child like that," Sophie argued. "If a handsome young captain wanted to come pay his addresses, I'd be interested. As it is, my most persistent suitor is just a stodgy old marquess."

Eleanor closed her eyes and rested her head against the door frame. The marquess may not be so very old, but stodgy definitely fit. Sophie had always been much more likely to fall for a dashing captain than for a fancy title. Taking a deep breath to compose herself, Eleanor pushed the door open. Sophie's head shot up, but before anyone could speak, she stalked over to the pianoforte, grabbed a piece of music at random, and began to play. Anne crossed to Eleanor at the door and tugged on Eleanor's arm. They slipped out, leaving Sophie to soothe her mood with music.

Chapter 12

Aunt Everley had kept her promise to only schedule four evening events each week, but this Saturday night they were to attend another ball that Aunt Everley could not justify declining. Eleanor expected Sophie to pester her when they were next alone about going to Faerie, but it was Anne who joined her in her room when they were changing to go for a walk the next day.

"I know you're worried about opening a gate during a party again," Anne said, "especially if Mr. Weston is there. But have you thought—how many weeks do we have left?"

"What do you mean?" Eleanor asked.

"I've seen the way you and Mr. Weston look at each other," Anne said. Eleanor blushed. "And Mr. Farrow..."

"Is bringing his daughter for you to meet," Eleanor finished for her. "He'll ask you soon."

Anne blushed and nodded. "I hope so."

"And if he asks you, you'll say yes and be happy?"

"More than happy," Anne said. "But you know the rule: we can't go to Faerie once we're engaged. We don't have many more weeks before we'll be cut off, and I can't afford to waste one."

Eleanor had expected to bring Anne over to her side of

the argument, but Anne succeeded in convincing her instead. Perhaps Mr. Weston wouldn't even be at this ball—they had many evening engagements where he wasn't present.

On Saturday evening, Eleanor's nerves were higher than they'd been all Season. Once she was dressed in her figured muslin, she went to Anne's room. She tried to fix her own hair in the mirror, but her hands were shaking too much.

"For heaven's sake," Anne said, putting her hands on Eleanor's shoulders and forcing her into a chair. She deftly twisted Eleanor's hair up and pinned it. "Good enough. I doubt you'll sit still for me to braid it."

Eleanor shook her head and jumped to her feet.

"Do your curls," Anne instructed, making way for Sophie to take the chair.

Eleanor wrapped a section of hair around her finger and thought the spell-word that would set the curl. Then she took another section and twisted it around her finger, but her nervous mind wandered off and she came back to herself a minute later, still twirling her finger through that one section of hair. She spelled the rest of the curls, frowning at herself in the mirror. Once she'd finished, however, she paced the room again.

Anne took her aside as they were grabbing their reticules and spencers. "We don't have many left," she murmured. "Make this one count."

Eleanor nodded and followed her sisters out of the room. She didn't like to hope Mr. Weston wouldn't be there, but it would definitely set her mind at ease.

The ballroom was bright, crowded, and noisy. Daylight still gleamed outside, and Eleanor made her way to one of the open windows after the second set. The weather had been glorious all week, and the air was just cool enough without being chill.

"No need to sneakily open a window," a voice said from behind her.

She blushed as she looked up to see Mr. Weston, his mouth quirked and teasing.

"I didn't think to see you so soon," Eleanor said when she could find her voice. "Did you know we would be here?"

"Not... exactly." A little color rose in his cheeks. "I do, however, occasionally take Lady Sterling's advice on what invitations to accept."

"I see," Eleanor said. "And she must have a good idea of what parties Aunt Everley will take us to."

He bowed slightly. "Are you offended?"

"Flattered." She smiled.

"Good," he said. "Because I believe you promised me a dance."

She took his offered arm. Her heart and mind were a flutter of nerves and excitement as they took their place on the floor. She saw Sophie preparing to dance, and the Earl of Tarrock too. He was with a tall blonde that Eleanor knew by sight but not by name, but he was watching Eleanor with a frown. Eleanor turned away from the others as Mr. Weston took one of her gloved hands in his. When he placed his other hand on the small of her back, her breath caught. Warmth from his hand sizzled through the thin muslin of her dress. Her heart raced. The room was suddenly much too hot.

Breathe, she told herself. *You can't dance if you're not breathing.*

The dance began. She had wondered once why Mr. Weston had never asked her for a waltz, and whether his limp would make the dance harder for him. But he led with confidence, and if his steps occasionally had a slight hesitation, it was more than made up for by the flutter of being so close. They ought to have talked while they were dancing, but Eleanor couldn't think of a single thing to say.

As Mr. Weston led her through a complicated turn, Eleanor noticed the briefest flinch cross his face. His limp was worse for several steps afterwards. She opened her mouth to ask if he was hurt and if he wanted to stop dancing and sit down, but before she could speak, he gave her the slightest shake of his head and smiled at her.

Smiled. <3

The sweet, heartfelt expression told her more clearly than words that he'd rather be here on this dance floor with her than anywhere else. She couldn't tear her eyes away. The nerves and excitement melted into nothing, and it was just this moment, and she didn't want to breathe. Was this what falling in love felt like?

The music stopped and after a few more steps so did they, but Eleanor didn't step back, and Mr. Weston didn't remove his hand. They stood smiling at each other for a breathless moment before they were interrupted by a gentleman clearing his throat.

Eleanor blinked and glanced over. Lord Tarrock bowed and said, "Forgive me for interrupting, Miss Eleanor, but may I have the next?"

Mr. Weston stepped back and dropped his hand from her waist. He brought her hand to his lips and then dropped that too. He bowed and disappeared into the crowd.

Eleanor danced the next several sets, but she was distracted and nervous again. It was nearly time to open the gate; another dance; her sisters appeared at her side. Eleanor cast the unnoticeable spell without saying a word, knowing that

CHAPTER 12

her sisters had already won the argument and that nothing Eleanor could say would change their minds. But she had a sick feeling in her stomach as they slipped out of the ballroom and found an empty room with a second door. Eleanor locked the door behind them, Sophie flitted around the room to set the chronology spell, and Anne opened the gate. It was too simple, too practiced. Eleanor followed her sisters onto the marble staircase, pulling the door shut behind her. She took a deep breath. She didn't want to ruin one of their last visits to Faerie by wishing she weren't there. A new spell idea had occurred to her tonight, and this was the perfect chance to ask Lady Snow about it. She strode purposefully down the steps after her sisters.

There.

James felt the first hint of magic and made his way out of the ballroom as quickly as he could without being impolite to the people he passed. He still hadn't come up with a good theory for why the same magic should be done at so many different balls in different houses, or why it was only Saturday nights but not every Saturday. His only hope of figuring it out was to get to the source and watch the magic itself. And this time he came prepared.

He located the locked door without trouble. It was held by the same spell as the last time. He spent a few minutes trying to dismantle the spell. When that failed, he placed his palm against the door and thought a spell-word, a new spell he'd adapted that would open anything that was spellbound. The lock clicked.

James pushed the door cautiously open. It was a study, with a large desk in the center and bookshelves lining the walls. It was dark and empty. James paced slowly around the room. There was another spell binding the whole room, but for what purpose, James couldn't guess. The rest of the magic concentrated around a door in the far corner. It was locked, and it refused to open, even with repeated uses of the new spell. James frowned. He'd just have to wait for the magicians to come out. He'd already used up six or seven minutes. Another five minutes and the magic would be over. He paced the room, keeping his eye on the door in the corner.

Five minutes. Ten. Twenty. Still the magic continued unchanged. James sank into a chair opposite the desk. His leg had been aching ever since that turn during the waltz.

His frown faded as he remembered dancing with Eleanor. She had made him lightheaded, with her waterfall-silver eyes and her scent of wildflowers and the way she smiled up at him. It had felt, for a few minutes, as if she only had eyes for him. And it was intoxicating.

He wished he'd been able to hide the pain when his knee almost gave out. No man wanted to appear weak before such a girl. But she'd never seemed to think less of him because of his injury, even when his leg made him such an indifferent dancer. She was so graceful herself, so light and easy in the dance, that she deserved better. She deserved someone hale and whole and unscarred. Like the Earl of Tarrock, who was also young and handsome and titled.

James scowled.

He hadn't come to town looking for a bride. He was content as a bachelor. Or he had been. Now he couldn't get Eleanor out of his head. <u>And the way she'd fit so perfectly in his arms while they danced… He couldn't help imagining how it would feel to pull her close and enfold her in his arms completely</u>.

Notice that this time he can still remember Eleanor even after the unnoticeable spell?

He blinked and checked his watch. Forty minutes. He got up and paced, then took a book off a shelf at random and sat back down. He used a spell-word to light the candle on the desk and began to read.

It was the most boring book he could have chosen, a history of agriculture in the midlands. His eyes glazed over as he read, and he dozed off.

James woke with a start and jumped to his feet. The book fell off his lap with a thud. Nothing had changed except that the candle had burned low. The spells were still there. He checked his watch—he'd been asleep for an hour. He began pacing again, limping worse until the muscles loosened up. Would anyone at the ball notice he'd been gone so long? Cole would, but he was busy making himself agreeable to Miss Young. Would Eleanor expect him to ask her for a second dance? The hope almost sent him back to the ballroom, but he stopped himself. He'd waited this long. He had to see what was going on here.

As they trotted up the staircase away from Faerie, Anne asked Eleanor what she'd spent so long talking to Lady Snow about.

"With so few visits left, I would have thought you'd have danced more."

Eleanor hadn't felt like dancing. Her Fae partners, too perfect in almost every respect, seemed vague and insipid and hollow. No one could compare to one partner at the ball she'd left behind.

She told her sisters about the new idea she'd had for a spell. Anne shot her a surprised look.

"Have you already reached enough of an understanding to be giving Mr. Weston gifts?"

Eleanor blushed. "No... not yet."

"But soon," Sophie teased. "I wouldn't be surprised if he called on Papa tomorrow. Or cornered him tonight."

Anne laughed at Eleanor's embarrassment. "He smiled at you, I saw it."

Eleanor thought it was high time to change the subject. "Anne, what was Lord River saying to you just before we left?"

Anne's smile fell. Eleanor reached the door and put her hand on the handle, but she paused, waiting for her sisters to catch up.

"He said I can only come once more," Anne said quietly.

"What?" Sophie shrieked.

CHAPTER 12

Eleanor's hand slipped and the door unlatched, hovering open an inch as she stared at her sisters.

"He told me I can only come once more," Anne repeated. "After that, the two of you must go alone."

Eleanor's heart sank. She'd known this was coming, but to have the end date so soon... She turned and pushed the door open.

There was someone in the room.

Gut-wrenching as it is, this was one of my favorite scenes to write.

Eleanor froze as she saw shock and horror dawn on Mr. Weston's face. All of the air seemed to vanish from the room. She couldn't breathe. She couldn't move.

"What—?" Anne began. She gasped, hesitated, then shoved Eleanor gently in the back to propel her forward.

Eleanor stumbled a few steps into the room. Her sisters came out after her, and she knew they were closing the door and ending their spells. She wasn't watching them, though. Her eyes were locked on Mr. Weston's, and her stomach dropped past her feet at the suspicion and hurt she saw there.

"What is this?" he whispered.

She couldn't answer. Three young ladies sneaking out of a ball without a chaperone—what must he think?

"What is this?" His voice, still hoarse, was stronger this time.

With a monumental effort, Eleanor approached him. She couldn't tell him everything, not now. It would take hours, and Sophie had already removed the chronology spell. Would he even listen? But she owed him the truth.

"Call on me Monday. Ask me to go driving. I'll tell you everything then." Barely more than a whisper, but she was surprised by how calm she sounded.

He said nothing, just gazed at her with deep, dark eyes. Her sisters repaired their slippers and gestured to her that it was time to go.

Eleanor took a deep breath and a step closer. She had to choke the words out. "I must ask that you not speak a word of this to anyone." She reached out, tentatively, and brushed her fingers along the end-of-day stubble on his jaw. She thought the spell-word to ensure his silence.

He flinched back from her touch, his appalled expression like a knife to her heart. A tear leaked down her cheek, and she fled with her sisters.

Chapter 13

James didn't return to the ballroom. He stood stunned for several minutes after the Miss Mayburys left, his mind and heart too full to move. Then suddenly he couldn't stay still a moment longer, and he strode out of the house, not bothering to call for the carriage. Lady Sterling and Cole would need it to get home, and while he could send it back for them, he really didn't want to be cooped up in anything right now. He was restless, and with plenty of anger and magic at hand, he was more than a match for any footpads.

As he stormed through town, he struggled to be rational, to allow for a misinterpretation of the circumstances. But the circumstances looked bad, no matter how he tried to view them. Three young ladies sneaking out of a ball on their own, late at night, without a chaperone? Opening a magical pathway to who-knew-where to meet God-only-knew-whom? Their reputations could be ruined by that alone.

Add to that Miss Maybury's statement just as they were opening the door. James had heard them and jumped to his feet, sick dread flooding him as he recognized the voices. Who was "he"? Who was the gentleman to whom she'd been referring? His stomach clenched at the thought of Eleanor with another man, turning that smile on anyone else.

And what about poor Farrow! Farrow would have to be warned before he offered for Miss Maybury. But James had been sworn to secrecy—no, he'd been *spelled* to secrecy. He flinched again at the memory of Eleanor's fingers trailing softly along his jaw. Earlier tonight he'd have died for a touch like that. Now it felt like another cut to the heart, that she didn't trust him. If she'd only asked for his word, he would have given it, however unwillingly. And how did she even *know* a spell like that?

A church bell tolled somewhere ahead, ringing the hour. James wasn't listening, but it caught his attention anyway. It was ringing too many times. He didn't catch the exact number—eleven? Twelve? That couldn't be right. He'd woken up from his accidental nap well past midnight, and he'd paced the study for another hour, waiting. Another church bell across town began tolling, and this time James counted. Eleven.

Impossible.

Then it struck him what the unknown spell binding the whole room had been. It had taken the room out of the flow of time. Hours could be spent in that room—or through a magical door opened in that room—and no time at all would have gone by in the rest of the world.

Under normal circumstances, the magic itself would have impressed him. But now it was tainted by wondering where Eleanor and her sisters could have learned it, and why— *why*—were they using it?

His only hope of answers was to call for her Monday, but by then she could easily have a convincing lie prepared. Would she even tell him the truth? And could he bear to be near her long enough to hear it? He didn't want to see her—Monday or ever—but his sense of justice insisted that he ought to. She ought to have a chance to explain herself, to clear up any misconceptions there might be. He owed her that much.

James paced the streets of London until his leg was ready to give out, then returned to his rooms and collapsed onto the bed, fully dressed, where he spent the rest of the night glaring at the dark ceiling.

Eleanor waited to remove the unnoticeable spell until she had taken the chair next to Aunt Everley where she sat with the other chaperones along the edge of the ballroom. Anne and Sophie positioned themselves nearby, and as soon as the spell dissolved, they fell into conversation with the people around them, as naturally as could be. Eleanor watched as gentlemen approached them for dances, gazing numbly as her sisters smiled and accompanied their partners to the floor. It was as if they'd had an entirely different experience than she had a few minutes ago. And they had—Mr. Weston had turned his pain-stricken eyes on Eleanor alone.

Lord Tarrock approached Eleanor and asked for a second dance. She excused herself, claiming she was tired and preferred to sit. Instead of leaving to find another partner, he took the chair beside her.

He frowned. "Are you unwell?"

"Perfectly well," Eleanor said, wishing her voice was steadier. "I'm just tired."

"Are you quite sure? You're as pale as your gown." He raised his voice to address Aunt Everley. "Isn't she pale, ma'am? I'm afraid she is not well."

Aunt Everley turned her full attention to Eleanor for the first time since she'd sat down. "You do look poorly, dear. Perhaps we should get you home."

"No, really, I'm well—" Eleanor protested, but the other two talked over her.

"How may I be of assistance? May I order your carriage?" the earl asked.

"That would be a great help, thank you," Aunt Everley said. She stood. "Let's find your father, dear."

Eleanor stood, uncomfortable with both sets of eyes on her. The earl offered his arm, and she took it because it would be rude not to, but she wished he would go away. They found Papa in the card room. He took one look at Eleanor and made over his cards to his neighbor. *Do I look that frail?* she thought. The Earl of Tarrock gave Eleanor into Papa's care and hurried off to order the carriage for them, while Aunt Everley, with a final injunction to go straight to bed, returned to the ballroom to stay with Anne and Sophie. Eleanor and Papa walked slowly down to where the carriage was just pulling around for them. Papa helped her into the carriage, made sure she was snug with blankets tucked around her, even though it was not chilly in the slightest, and asked no questions.

Once at home, Eleanor went straight to bed as instructed. Papa sent Sarah up with tea, but Eleanor couldn't swallow it. She lay in bed, unable to get comfortable or close her eyes. Her sisters came home hours later with Aunt Everley. Her aunt peeked into her room to see if she was sleeping, but Eleanor had closed the curtains on the fourposter bed, and her aunt left without a word. A few minutes later, Anne tiptoed into the room, pushing the curtain aside. Eleanor closed her eyes and slowed her breathing, pretending to sleep until she heard her sister's footsteps move back toward the door and the click of the latch as it closed behind her. Eleanor wasn't ready to talk to Anne about what had happened. She didn't know what to think, let alone what to say.

What must Mr. Weston think of them, of her? She couldn't stop thinking about the hurt in his eyes, the betrayal, the shock. How he jerked away from the touch of her hand. Tears came, and Eleanor did nothing to stop them. She wept until she'd soaked her pillow, then, feeling hollow, she got out of bed and paced the room.

She'd tell him the truth, the whole truth, even though Mama had impressed on them as she died that their connection with Faerie was a particular secret. Lord River had stressed secrecy as well, forbidding them from ever bringing human guests with them to Faerie. The Fae valued privacy and were mostly indifferent to human concerns; if word got out that they could be contacted, they would never have a moment's peace. People would want the Fae to magically solve all their problems. And by extension, Eleanor and her sisters would be bombarded with requests for magical solutions beyond the scope of their abilities.

But Mr. Weston knew some of their secret by now anyway, and whatever else he suspected must be infinitely worse than the truth. Eleanor knew she could count on him to keep their secret. She wept again at the necessity of the silencing spell tonight, but what if, in his emotion, he let something slip? What if his suspicions somehow got to Aunt Everley or Mr. Farrow or someone else in the *ton*?

Eleanor didn't bother getting back into bed until the sky outside her window showed the telltale lightening of dawn. Then the hours of dancing and magic and sleeplessness and tears caught up with her. She fell asleep, and she stayed asleep through checks from Sarah, her aunt, and her sisters. She woke up, was miserable and headachy, rolled over, and went back to sleep. She woke again at dinnertime, but she wasn't hungry, so she rang for tea.

Later, Anne came and sat with her. By then, Eleanor was in her dressing gown in a chair by the window. Her sister silently took the opposite chair and watched the sun set. After a long time, Anne said, "Just tell him the truth. He's not a fool. He'll understand."

"And if he doesn't?" Eleanor asked faintly.

"Then Lord Tarrock would be glad to take his place, if your heart can find room for him."

Anne gave her a hug, kissed her cheek, and left. As soon as she was gone, Eleanor's tears began again, and she sobbed for several minutes. At least Anne had not tried to convince her to lie. She already had her mind made up, but it was a relief not to argue. But she found no comfort from the conversation. At length, she calmed her breathing, dried her eyes, and went back to bed.

Chapter 14

Eleanor was up in time for breakfast the next morning. She carefully washed her face and brushed her hair, sitting perfectly still for Sarah to braid it and pin it up. The day dress she chose was simple, green with cream stripes. She laid her bonnet, gloves, and pelisse on the bed so that she wouldn't need to look for them later. She checked the mirror one more time, then joined her family in the breakfast room.

"How are you feeling, Eleanor?" Papa asked, looking up from his newspaper.

"Much better," she said. "I just needed sleep, I think."

"You still look a bit wan. Have some toast." Aunt Everley passed her the plate.

Eleanor ate, knowing that her family was watching and that she hadn't eaten since dinner on Saturday, but still without much appetite. Only copious amounts of tea enabled her to swallow the dry toast. But she knew that if she didn't eat, there was no way she could convince her aunt that she was well enough to go driving with Mr. Weston.

"I think fresh air would do Eleanor good," Anne said mildly.

Aunt Everley agreed. "Fresh air cures most ailments."

"Perhaps we should go walking this morning," Sophie suggested.

"No indeed," their aunt said. "Eleanor is still much too weak to walk out."

"Maybe a drive, then?" Anne suggested.

Eleanor choked on her toast and gulped at her tea. Papa lowered his paper and looked at her. When it was clear that Eleanor was not in any further danger from her food, he said, "I have business in town this morning, but perhaps after dinner, if Eleanor is feeling well enough."

The subject changed, and Eleanor breathed a sigh of relief. She shot Anne a look across the table. Anne just smiled innocently.

They retired to the sitting room. Eleanor forced herself to join in the conversation, but she wasn't in the mood for more than a few brief sentences. She occupied herself by looking through the rag bag of fabric scraps for something that would work for the project she'd been discussing with Lady Snow. Not that she was likely to need it any time soon, given the expression she'd seen on Mr. Weston's face the other night. She may not need it at all, depending on how today's conversation went. She chose not to think about that, however, burrowing instead into the rag bag. She found a strip of green silk left over from hemming the dress she'd worn at Aunt Everley's dinner party. It was not quite two hands-breadths wide, but it was a full yard long. She stashed it in her work basket for later. Acceptable calling hours had begun, and she would be too restless to sew until Mr. Weston came. And what if he didn't come? Eleanor rose abruptly and walked about the room.

Half an hour later, a footman appeared at the sitting room door, announcing that Mr. Weston was in the drawing room. Aunt Everley immediately rose. Anne and Sophie did as well, and the three girls followed their aunt down the hall. Anne took Eleanor's hand, and Sophie gave her arm a squeeze. Eleanor was grateful for her sisters' support, because Mr. Weston's face was uncharacteristically grave when they entered the room. Aunt Everley didn't seem to notice anything beyond his usual solemnity. She welcomed him graciously, and he bowed and commented on the fine weather.

"Indeed," Aunt Everley agreed. "It has been very fine for the past fortnight, and today may be the most mild of all."

"I had hoped—I had hoped Miss Eleanor might go for a drive in the park with me this morning."

Eleanor had the impression that Mr. Weston was as uncomfortable as she was.

Aunt Everley brightened. "We were just saying this morning that fresh air would do Eleanor a world of good. She hasn't been quite well since the ball, you know." Mr. Weston shot a quick glance at Eleanor, but she couldn't read the look. "Eleanor, why don't you get your bonnet? It is very kind of Mr. Weston to drive out with you this morning, I'm sure."

Anne squeezed her hand, and Eleanor was out the door in an instant. She put on the things she'd laid on the bed, adjusted her bonnet in the mirror, and was back in the drawing room within minutes. Mr. Weston bowed to them all and escorted her down to his curricle, which waited by the front door. He handed her up, climbed up beside her, and set the horses walking toward Hyde Park.

Neither of them spoke until they were well out of earshot of the house.

"What was your aunt saying about you being ill?" Mr. Weston asked.

"It was nothing," Eleanor said. "I... didn't sleep on Saturday night and spent the day abed yesterday. Anne... helpfully suggested this morning that fresh air would do me good."

Silence stretched long, and Eleanor wondered how to break it. She had no idea what to say or where to begin. So it was with relief and alarm that she heard Mr. Weston's first words.

"Who is he?" The words came out hoarse and forced, as if he didn't want to know.

"I beg your pardon?"

"I overheard your eldest sister mentioning a gentleman the other night, who said that she could only come back once more. Who is he?"

Eleanor's mouth fell open. She hadn't realized just how bad an idea he'd gotten. "He's our grandfather," she said.

Mr. Weston's face was stony. "Do not lie to me, Miss Maybury. Your father and your uncle Kerring have their titles because both of your grandfathers are dead."

Eleanor ignored the callousness of his words. "The former Viscount of Kerring was not my mother's father," she said softly. "Her father was a Faerie, and he is very much alive."

Mr. Weston's head jerked around to stare at her. "I beg your pardon?"

Eleanor sighed. "It's a long story."

"I have all the time in the world."

"When Mama was twelve years old, her mother fell ill. Before she died, she told Mama the terrible secret. She didn't know who Mama's father truly was, but he could only have been a Faerie to have deceived her as he did. He came to Mama a year later, and he showed her how to open a gate to Faerie, and he brought her there to dance at the Faerie Queen's ball each Seventh Night. She went every week until she became engaged to Papa. When we were young, she told us stories about Faerie, and she taught us magic. Three months after she died, our grandfather came for us. He taught us the spells we'd need to come to the Seventh Night balls, and he has been our escort each week ever since."

"You're telling me that you've been going dancing with strangers without parental permission since before you were old enough to be out in Society?"

"No-o," Eleanor said slowly. "We had Mama's permission, and we were escorted by our grandfather. And Anne was sixteen, so she, at least, was out."

Mr. Weston gave her a sidelong look that said he wasn't satisfied with her explanations so far. "Presuming I believe that you have Faerie blood," and from his expression, Eleanor could tell it was a very big presumption, "what does that mean for you? Do you have Fae magic?"

"Aside from the invitation to Seventh Night, it means very little. It might have impacted Mama more, but my sisters and I are mostly human. Our magic is the same as yours. But... a magical gift is an aptitude, is it not? Like being a gifted musician or artist? We have a greater aptitude than most. An affinity, one might say."

Lady Snow had explained that to Eleanor during one of their very first visits to Faerie, when Eleanor was still trying to process the ramifications of their unexpected bloodline. Eleanor had built on that aptitude by years of devoted practice, but Lady Snow professed that even Sophie at age thirteen, who prior to the lure of Faerie had had to be cajoled to practice magic, was capable of spells that would stump Oxford graduates. Charles and Henry, too, had already shown a giftedness if not an interest in magic.

Mr. Weston considered this, frowning. After a moment, he

said, "Very well. Tell me about your trips into Faerie."

He said it as though he were humoring her, which rankled a bit, but Eleanor was grateful that he was listening and giving her the chance to explain. So she told him about the spells they used, and about the marble staircase that took them from the gate to the colonnade. She told him about the dancers and Lord River and Lady Snow. "But before we can join the dance, we always greet Her Majesty."

"Her Majesty?"

"The Faerie Queen," Eleanor said. "She's gone by many names, I believe, but the two I know are Titania and Hera. We see her every Seventh Night. Her consort—he goes by Oberon or Zeus, among other things—only comes once a year, at the summer solstice."

"Zeus and Hera?" Mr. Weston's voice had a sharp, mocking edge. "Are you trying to tell me now that you dance with the gods of the Ancient Greeks? This is the outside of enough, Miss Maybury."

"Not at all," Eleanor said, wishing she could keep the quaver out of her voice. He was responding as any rational man would. She felt tears—how could she have any left by now?—aching at the corners of her eyes. "We dance with the Faeries, who, when they were seen by the Greeks, were called gods. But they've never called themselves that."

I don't know when it occurred to me to have the Faeries also be the Greek gods, but I love how well it works.

CHAPTER 14

Mr. Weston grunted and waved his hand. "Go on. Tell me the rest."

Eleanor took a deep breath and told him about repairing their shoes when they got home, and about Mama's tradition of no social visits on Sunday, and how they'd kept it so that they could rest after their unnaturally long night.

"Was it your grandfather who taught you how to separate a room from the stream of time?"

"Yes. An hour in the room only lasts a minute or two out of it."

"You've told me about three spells—the door, the room, and the gate," he said. "There was another, a spell that you cast before the others and you dissolved after. What was that?"

Eleanor smiled faintly. "That was one of Mama's. It makes you unnoticeable."

"How so?"

"I cast it over the three of us in a ballroom. No one notices us leaving, and no one thinks about us while we're gone. It's as if we simply don't exist in their minds during that time."

"Show me."

Eleanor blinked at him. "I don't know if it will work on you. It doesn't on my sisters."

"Because we're magicians? Or because they're part Fae?"

"Neither. <u>Because I'm already too rooted in your—consciousness.</u>" A few days ago she might have said "heart," <u>but today she couldn't.</u> "My sisters and I are too close. It would be like trying not to notice one of your arms or legs."

"Show me anyway." They were no longer moving, the curricle stopped in the flow of traffic. Mr. Weston turned to face her completely.

Eleanor nodded and thought the spell-word. Mr. Weston frowned. Eleanor ended the spell.

"I didn't really think it would work on you," she said with a small shrug.

"Not now," he agreed. "Not while you have my full attention."

It looked like he was thinking about something, but he said no more about it. Eleanor thought there was a good chance that she could have cast the spell when he was not paying attention and it still would have had no effect on him. They finished the loop of the park. As they passed through the park gate to go home, Eleanor broke the silence.

"I know I can count on your discretion," she said. "This secret has been known only to my sisters and myself since our mother died. My father and my aunt don't even know."

"I'm honored by your trust in me." His voice was laced with a hint of sarcasm. "Although I think you can enforce my silence."

Heat rushed to Eleanor's face. "I'm sorry. I was afraid—" Her unshed tears choked her. She swallowed hard. "That spell wore off yesterday. I won't use it again. I was afraid that you might accidentally let something slip to Mr. Cole or…."

"Or Mr. Farrow, who might have lost interest in your sister."

Eleanor nodded. "I wanted you to know the whole truth first. And… I wanted to let Anne decide how much of our secret to share with Mr. Farrow."

Mr. Weston pulled the curricle to a stop in front of the house and sighed. "You have my word—I will not speak a syllable about your secret to another soul without your permission."

"Thank you." Eleanor met his eyes. The horror and shock

that she'd seen on Saturday night were gone, but she couldn't miss the hurt and doubt. "And thank you for allowing me to explain."

He bowed, and she climbed down. She went to the door and paused on the front step to look back. He nodded solemnly to her and drove away. Eleanor sighed and went inside, straight to her bedroom to take off her bonnet and pelisse. She sat down by the window. The conversation had gone as well as could be expected, and she knew she had nothing to be disappointed in. But Eleanor was sure her aunt expected her to receive a proposal while she was driving alone with Mr. Weston. That thought was enough to require a few minutes to cry and compose herself before going downstairs to join the family.

James pulled the curricle into the yard of the boarding house and turned the horses over to one of the grooms. He strode up to his rooms, packed a bag, and scribbled a note to George Cole. He gave the note to a servant to deliver. Once back in the curricle, he drove out of town. London was suffocating. He needed to get away from the balls and dinner parties, away from Eleanor and her preposterous story. Away from her eyes and her smile and the tear he'd seen stealing down her cheek. He needed to think; he would rather do anything *but* think.

Chapter 15

The next morning, Eleanor and Sophie were in the sitting room when Harvey announced that a gentleman was in the drawing room. Eleanor rose immediately, her sister not far behind. They arrived just as Anne and Aunt Everley were coming from the breakfast room. Eleanor tried to suppress the hope that flared within her, but she knew her sisters saw her face fall when their guest turned out to be Mr. Farrow, not Mr. Weston. Anne stepped forward to greet him. Eleanor tried to be happy for her sister's sake, but her heart hurt too much.

He only stayed with them a quarter hour, talking of indifferent things. He had just been in Essex, and he talked of the roads and the events of the previous Sunday. He seemed more restless than usual, and it became more pronounced the longer he stayed. At last, he sat forward.

"Miss Maybury, I didn't return from Essex alone. Would you do me the honor of calling on Thursday and meeting Miss Farrow?"

Anne smiled. "I hadn't thought you'd bring her to town so soon. I'd be delighted."

He held her eyes, his own smile brightening as if he saw all his hopes answered there. Eleanor watched the exchange with a wistfulness that stole her breath. Beside her, Sophie's fingers fisted in her skirt, and Eleanor glanced at her, startled to see a tight jaw and a furrowed brow.

Mr. Farrow tore his eyes from Anne, said his farewells, and rose. Anne rose as well and walked with him out to the entrance hall, and Aunt Everley followed them.

As soon as they were gone, Eleanor went to the door and closed it, then turned to Sophie.

"Do you have something against Mr. Farrow?"

Sophie scowled. "He's nice enough."

"Then why are you—"

"You don't see it, do you?" Sophie snapped.

Eleanor blinked at her. "Don't see what?"

"Mr. Farrow is going to propose to Anne any day now," Sophie said slowly, as if spelling out the simplest thing to someone incurably stupid. "And then you will marry Mr. Weston."

Eleanor winced. "You can't know that," she interrupted, "not after—"

"Oh, please!" Sophie burst. "The man is over head and ears in love with you! If he turns his back because of this one thing, he's an idiot."

"Men have done stupider things."

Sophie gave her a disgusted look. "You're still missing the point because you can't see past yourself. You two are going to get married, and I'll be left alone."

Eleanor gaped. "But I'm sure Lord Linfield will offer—"

"I don't want to marry Lord Linfield!"

"If not the marquess, you'll have other offers, other suitors you like better."

"I don't know if I want to get married at all." Sophie was on her feet now, glaring at her. "I definitely don't want to be stuck here alone with Papa and Aunt Everley while I wait and wonder if my ideal gentleman even exists. Finding a husband means losing Faerie for good—you know the rules! I would have to be completely, epically... *legendarily* in love to risk that."

Eleanor stared at her sister as tears leaked from Sophie's eyes.

"Why can't everything just stay the way it is?"

"But, Sophie..." Eleanor held out her hands, helpless.

"Your lives are coming together perfectly, and I'm happy for you, I'm sure." Sophie's tears and her dark scowl spoke more truth than her words. "But did you ever think to notice that my life is going to pieces?" She stalked from the room.

Eleanor gaped after her. She had known that Sophie wasn't as eager to get married and settle down as Anne, and it was not a revelation that Lord Linfield was not a perfect match. But she hadn't realized that Sophie didn't want to get married at all. Eleanor had never seen the end of their trips to Faerie as a choice—marriage was a foregone conclusion, wasn't it? For her and Anne it had been, and she'd thought for Sophie too.

Guilt tugged at Eleanor's heart for being so wrapped up in her own emotional mess that she didn't see the pain she'd been causing her sister. She walked slowly back to the sitting room and sat alone by the window. She began to hem the edges of the strip of green silk as she let her mind wander. She remembered Sophie's excitement the first time Lord River had come to take them to Faerie. Sophie had never applied herself to lessons—other than Greek and music—with much enthusiasm, but she'd practiced magic almost as diligently as Eleanor when they were taught the spells to open the gate and repair their shoes. The three of them had always been close, but they'd developed an even stronger bond after Mama passed and they began their weekly adventures. No wonder it hurt Sophie to see Anne and Eleanor ready to move on. They would always be close, and they'd always have the shared secret, but things *would* change. Anne already had only one visit left. How many would Eleanor have beyond that? And would it still be any fun for Sophie, to go without her sisters?

Eleanor sighed. Mama had gone alone. She'd never had anyone to share the secret with. Eleanor remembered the night Mama had told them about her own mother's deathbed confession. Grandmother had fallen ill with a wasting fever when Mama was only twelve years old. She had spoken to each of her children privately, but to Mama she'd revealed her deepest, darkest secret: thirteen years earlier, the Viscount of Kerring, her husband, had gone away on business. He'd returned two days before they'd expected him, and Grandmother had welcomed him home as a wife should. The next morning, he was gone, and no one else could remember that he'd even been there. This made Grandmother uneasy, and she remembered thinking that her husband had looked too perfect the night before, but she'd thought it was only that she'd missed him so badly. The Viscount arrived home a day later, right on time, looking as dirty and weary as any man who has spent several days on the road. Grandmother gave birth to Mama nine months later, not knowing for sure who the father was. But, she told Mama, only a Faerie could have played such a trick, and <u>Mama was her only child with Fae eyes.</u>

<u>Mama's eyes were gray shot through with silver, just like Eleanor's.</u>

Grandmother died without breathing a word of her secret

to anyone but Mama. Mama never told anyone until she confessed it all to her daughters on her own deathbed.

"The stories I've told you… they're all true," she'd said, her weak voice little more than a whisper. "I don't know when, or even if, Lord River will come for you. He came to me the first time when I was thirteen. Promise me that if he does come, you'll keep the secret and you won't be afraid."

He'd come three months later, the Seventh Night after Sophie's thirteenth birthday, when they were all old enough to go together.

They'd all slept restlessly since Mama's passing. Barely a night passed without Henry crying and Anne getting up to comfort him. The grief, the ache, the loss—Eleanor felt Mama's passing like physical pain, and she couldn't get comfortable in bed.

Then there he'd been, standing by the window, illuminated by the full moon, his silver eyes practically glowing.

"Sophie," she'd hissed.

"Yes," Sophie had whispered.

They lay in bed, staring at their Fae visitor. The spell was broken as Anne opened the door and closed it behind her with a sigh. When Eleanor looked over at her, she'd said, "He's asleep again. Hopefully, he'll stay—"

Then Anne's eyes landed on the gentleman by the window, and she'd fallen silent.

"Greetings, children," Lord River had said in his melodious voice.

"Lord River," Eleanor had whispered.

He looked at her, a smile playing on his lips. "Your mother told you about me? Good. Will you come and dance?"

In a daze, Eleanor had found herself on her feet with her

sisters, suddenly dressed for a ball that in England she'd be too young to attend.

"What about the boys?" Anne had asked.

"They are too young to visit Faerie," Lord River said. "Once they are old enough, they may come through the gate but not to dance. Her Majesty's invitation extends to my daughters alone."

Eleanor felt a twinge at the unfairness of this, but then Lord River was teaching them the spell to open the gate, and she forgot all about it as she followed him into Faerie for their first ball.

She'd wondered later, after the haze of grief had lifted, why Lord River had tricked her grandmother. Mama hadn't said, and Eleanor never had the courage to ask. She could only assume that Grandmother, if she looked anything like Mama, had been too great a beauty to resist.

Eleanor and her sisters had gone to Faerie every week in the five years since that first visit, missing only when they were ill until the two weeks they'd skipped when moving to Aunt Everley's house in town for this Season. Their adolescence had been one big shared secret, always the three of them, together.

The next morning, Sophie jumped at the chance to go shopping in Bond Street with Aunt Everley. Anne and Eleanor were staying home in case of callers, and it couldn't have been clearer that Sophie wanted to avoid them. Mr. Weston didn't come, and between the coldness of her sister and the absence of the gentleman, Eleanor had herself so twisted into knots that she couldn't concentrate on anything.

Aunt Everley bustled into the sitting room when they returned from shopping. Sophie was more subdued, and she looked at Eleanor uneasily as she took off her bonnet.

"We saw Lady Sterling today in Bond Street, just leaving the milliner's," Aunt Everley said, pulling off her gloves.

Eleanor froze.

"She mentioned that Mr. Weston had been called away suddenly on business to his country house on Monday. He must have left after taking you driving, Eleanor. Did he say anything about it to you?"

Eleanor felt the blood drain from her face. She managed the smallest shake of her head. Aunt Everley continued talking, but Eleanor didn't hear her. Anne's hand found hers and held it tight. After a few deep breaths, Eleanor got to her feet, mumbled an excuse, and escaped to her room. She flopped face down on her bed and let the emptiness overtake her.

<u>He was gone. He'd left town to avoid seeing her.</u>

<u>Could his feelings be plainer? He couldn't believe her, couldn't forgive the lies and secrets. Even if he did believe her, he obviously had no desire for a part-Fae wife.</u>

The tears came again, soaking into the coverlet. Eleanor had cried more over the past week than she had since Mama's passing. What was it about Mr. Weston that wreaked such havoc on her?

Love, obviously. She'd thought she might be falling in love when they danced, but she didn't realize she was so far gone. <u>Now the thought of never seeing him again, of spending her whole life without him, was intolerable. And worse, for him</u>

to hate her...

Eleanor didn't go down to dinner. Anne knocked at her door, but Eleanor mumbled something that was supposed to come out "please leave me alone." It was too muffled by the blankets to be real words, but Anne went away, and no one bothered her for the rest of the night.

The next morning, Eleanor washed her face and dressed with care. She would pretend, for her family's sake, that she was not dying inside. After all, Papa and Aunt Everley knew nothing about what had happened on Saturday night or Monday morning. To them, Mr. Weston's business in the country must be nothing serious, just something for him to deal with before returning to town, and her disappointment could only be at the loss of his company for a short time. She avoided looking at her sisters at breakfast. They knew; their sympathy would cause her to lose what precious little composure she had.

Anne and Aunt Everley prepared to call on Mr. Farrow, and when they left, Sophie called to Harvey.

"Eleanor and I are indisposed for visitors today," she said firmly. "Please turn all callers away."

Eleanor was grateful to her sister. They spent the morning in the sitting room in companionable silence, which warmed Eleanor's heart after Sophie's studied avoidance the day before.

They were still in the sitting room when Anne and Aunt Everley returned. Anne joined them immediately, while their aunt went to speak with the housekeeper. Eleanor asked what Anne thought of Miss Farrow, and while her question showed less eager curiosity than it might have a week ago, Anne answered as if it lacked nothing. Anne seemed to be bubbling over, and her news soon spilled out: she was engaged to Mr. Farrow.

In the first draft, I included the whole proposal scene from Anne's POV. It's now available as bonus content if you join my newsletter.

Eleanor rushed over to hug her sister. She and Sophie both wished Anne happy and assured her how delighted they were. Eleanor was glad to see that Sophie's smile was genuine, if a little strained; her own face hurt with the effort. Anne had just finished telling them the details when Aunt Everley entered.

"Girls," their aunt said, frowning at the calling cards in her hand, "why did you not receive visitors today? Lord Tarrock called."

Eleanor's smile fled, and her throat felt tight. "Headache," she squeaked. "I'm going to go lie down until dinner." She hurried past her aunt and up the stairs, catching her aunt's comment to her sisters that she did look pale and unwell.

She *felt* pale and unwell. Eleanor took refuge in her room, but she didn't lie down. She curled up in the armchair by the window, hugging her knees. She was happy for Anne, truly she was. Mr. Farrow was a good man, kind and honorable and loyal and amiable. She was sure he and her sister would be happy together and do good things in their parish. But she had an idea now of how Sophie had felt. As much as she wanted Anne to be happy, Eleanor felt like her stomach had

CHAPTER 15

turned to lead, and her eyes ached from the tears she didn't want to shed again. She wished so badly that she had been the one giving good news to her sisters, that she and Mr. Weston had been the ones who had come to an agreement.

But it was no use wishing. He was gone.

Eleanor went down to dinner with the family, but her father and aunt sent her back up to bed as soon as she'd finished eating. She didn't even have to ask the next morning; Aunt Everley insisted that she rest all day. She nodded silently and curled up in the sitting room with a book.

Her sisters joined her. She wasn't really reading, so she saw the looks they gave her book and then each other. Anne picked up Eleanor's workbasket and set it beside the chair.

"Finish it," Anne murmured. "He'll come back."

"I already told you he'd be an idiot not to," Sophie added.

Eleanor looked helplessly at them, a lump in her throat, but she set her book aside. She picked up the green silk. She'd already finished hemming the edges. She threaded a needle with purple silk and began to take slow, careful stitches. Her sisters were kind enough to turn away and not notice when she wiped her sleeve across her eyes.

Lord Tarrock called again that day, and Lord Linfield. Eleanor was left alone while the others sat with their guests. Lord Tarrock didn't stay long, but he left his well wishes for Eleanor and hoped she'd be feeling better the next day. Eleanor heard this message from her aunt and determined to be indisposed—she was certain her pallor wouldn't abate for several more days, and she was also certain that she couldn't bear to be cheerful and polite to any gentleman at the moment but one.

The next morning, Saturday, Aunt Everley took one look at

Eleanor and declared that they would not attend Lady York's party that evening after all, nor would Eleanor receive visitors that morning.

"I really think, dear, that you hadn't ought to have gone driving on Monday." She frowned her concern at Eleanor. "You hadn't been quite well on Sunday, and I think your outing may have prolonged your illness."

Eleanor could think of nothing to protest. She didn't regret the drive with Mr. Weston at all. In fact, if he called today, she'd argue until she was blue in the face to be allowed to drive out with him. But her aunt's concern had its uses. She didn't particularly want to go to the party tonight. She had nothing to fear now, opening a gate in another house, with Mr. Weston not present to notice, but she couldn't face conversing with any of the other gentlemen of the *ton*.

They were to stay home. She had another day of privacy. That was enough.

Chapter 16

Eleanor promised herself not to let her emotions color their last trip to Faerie together. She sensed something similar from Sophie, only in her younger sister it was a kind of desperation, clinging to this one last perfect night of youth. They dressed more carefully than usual, taking extra pains with their hair, jewelry, and gowns. Sophie locked the door, Eleanor set the chronology spell, and Anne opened the gate through the wardrobe. They clasped hands more tightly than they had in the five years since their first visits and followed Anne through the doorway. They descended the lantern-lit marble staircase and hurried along the passage, not pausing until they emerged into the wide colonnade.

They filed through the crowd around Her Majesty to make their curtsies.

"Welcome, children," she said with a smile. "Enjoy the ball, and come back to me before you leave."

She waved a graceful hand, and a path parted through the crowd for the three of them to approach the meadow full of dancers. Lord River waited for them at the edge of the marble courtyard. He bowed silently and offered his hand to Anne. She let go of Eleanor and went with him. A moment later, two more tall, elegant gentlemen appeared. Eleanor accepted Lord

Orion's arm, glad of a familiar face.

They danced for hours, spinning from partner to partner in an exhilarating rush. Eleanor saw Lady Snow watching among the spectators, but for once she had no desire to discuss magic. She didn't want to think about the spell they'd designed last week nor admit that it would never be needed.

Her friend found her, however, as the last song ended and she looked for her sisters. The Faerie's ice-blue eyes locked onto hers, and Eleanor had to tilt her head up as Lady Snow stepped close.

"Finish the spell, child," Lady Snow said quietly. "<u>Never leave a new spell unfinished or the next one you try may not work.</u> I won't be able to help you forever."

Then the lady walked away into the crowd, and Sophie and Anne hurried over.

"It's time," Anne whispered, clutching at both of their hands.

They approached the Queen, aware of her eyes on them long before they reached the front of the gathered Fae. They curtsied again, and when they rose, Her Majesty fixed Anne with her gaze.

"This was your last visit," she said. "You are no longer a child. The gate will not open for you again."

Anne bowed her head. "Thank you, Your Majesty, for letting me come for as long as you have. It has been an honor and a pleasure to join your revelries."

The Queen smiled. "We have enjoyed your visits, and we wish you well." She nodded and they were dismissed to walk back across the colonnade and up the passage for home.

Eleanor felt the high of dancing fade, and by the time they reached the top of the stairs, they were all trudging dejectedly. They sat on the edge of Eleanor's bed, repairing their shoes as they had so many times before. Sophie didn't look at her sisters as she jumped to her feet and ran out of the room. Anne looked after her.

"What—"

"Everything's changing," Eleanor said. "She doesn't like it."

"Is that why she's avoided Mr. Farrow all week?"

Eleanor nodded. "It's nothing against him."

Anne sighed. "I don't want things to change either…"

"Yes, you do," Eleanor reassured her. "You have a whole wonderful life ahead of you."

Anne smiled sadly. "It just hurts that to get that future I have to leave the past behind."

Eleanor laughed humorlessly. "I think that's how life works."

She hugged her sister and took down the last spell on her room as Anne snuck out the door. Once she was alone, she sat in the chair by the window for a few minutes. Her future didn't look as bright as Anne's, but at least she had more time to go to Faerie with Sophie.

By Monday morning, Eleanor was sick of moping. She felt wrung out and empty, and she had little energy or appetite, but enough was enough. Sophie was in a funk of her own, only leaving the pianoforte for meals. Anne and Aunt Everley were to spend the day with Lady Farrow, who had come to town to meet her son's betrothed. Eleanor was on her own, and she knew just what to do.

She called Sarah to her room to help her into a walking dress, then sent the maid to find seeds.

"Any vegetable will do," she instructed.

Sarah returned with folded paper packets labeled with drawings of produce. Eleanor pocketed them and tied on her bonnet.

"Where are we going, Miss Eleanor?" Sarah pulled on her gloves.

"Kittering's Home. Did you notice the empty window boxes when we were there?"

"I did, miss. Noticed there was still plenty of dirt in them, but it didn't look like they've seen flowers in a while."

"Exactly. I intend to put those boxes to use."

Mother Kittering was delighted to see Eleanor. Sarah made herself useful to Lissy in the kitchen again while Robert and Celeste joined Eleanor at the window in the schoolroom. Eleanor heaved the sash up while her two redheaded assistants looked on.

"Are we doing magic again, Miss Eleanor?" Celeste asked.

"We are." Eleanor pulled one of the seed packets from her pocket. Lettuce. She shook a few seeds from the packet into her palm and held them out to the children. "We're going to plant these in the window box. Bury them an inch or two under the dirt."

Robert and Celeste complied, neither of them fussing about getting their hands dirty. As they finished, the little boy named Connor ran up with a small watering pot, sloshing water out of it as he skidded to a halt.

"Sorry, miss." He looked with chagrin at the wet spot on Eleanor's skirt.

"No harm done. Would you like to water the seeds we just

planted?"

Connor carefully lifted the watering pot, sprinkling liquid over the window box.

"That's enough," Eleanor said. "Thank you."

Then, with three sets of eager eyes on her, she spoke the spell word to make the seeds grow, the same word she'd used to grow violets at Aunt Everley's dinner party. She remembered Mr. Weston's admiration of her spell work with a pang, but she swallowed back the emotion and watched the lettuces sprout and grow until they were about half their full size.

"I usually use this spell with flowers," she said, considering the vegetables. "They'll need to grow a bit on their own, but we've given them a good head start. Shall we plant some more?"

They continued on to the next window box where they planted more lettuce. Carrots were in the next two boxes. There were eight windows facing the square, and eight boxes to fill. Two received squash. Robert and Celeste each spoke the spell-word over one of those. The final two boxes were trickier, as peas and beans both wanted something to climb. Eleanor debated growing more carrots and squash instead, but she decided to give the beans a try. As she spoke the spell-word, she focused hard on the vines. They twined together as they grew, finding gaps in the brick around the window to grip.

"When you grow anything with vines, you'll want to concentrate on where the vines are growing as you say the spell," she told her helpers. She spoke the spell-word on the peas in the final box, and the vines curled around the window just like the beans had.

Eleanor dusted her hands. "There. Now you'll have fresh vegetables. I'll leave the seeds with Lissy so that you know where to find them when you're ready to plant more."

Robert looked awestruck. "You mean we can grow them ourselves?"

Eleanor's face felt stiff after so long without smiling, but Robert's innocent wonder drew one from her anyway. "Of course you can. Why do you think I taught you the spell-word? You know how to do it, so now you get to help feed everyone. Do you think you can handle the responsibility?"

"Yes, ma'am," Robert and Celeste said solemnly together.

"Yes'm," agreed Connor, who clutched the now-empty watering pot to his chest.

"Good," Eleanor said, meeting each of their eyes. "I'm counting on you, and so is Mother Kittering. And if you need help for any reason, send word to me with Lady Everley. All right?"

The children nodded. Eleanor dismissed them to wash their hands, then headed for the kitchen to give Lissy the seeds and gather Sarah. The magic had exhausted her, and she felt emotionally worn down, but a small portion of the weight that pressed against her heart had eased.

Eleanor's outing had gone unnoticed by her family, but her color had apparently improved enough that Aunt Everley saw no need to keep them home any longer. That night, they attended an evening party at Colonel Hastings'. The following night, they went to a concert with Mrs. Graham and her daughter. Lord Tarrock saw them there and joined them in their box during intermission to inquire after Eleanor's health, having missed her the past three times he'd called. She admitted that she had been unwell.

"I hope you're feeling better," he said. "You do look a bit peaked."

Eleanor was spared the need to respond to this by Aunt Everley and Mrs. Graham pressing Lord Tarrock to join them. He readily agreed, seating himself by Eleanor. To this point, she had had little interest in the concert, but she pretended to be listening attentively, because it spared her from carrying on a conversation with her neighbor. It wasn't that she disliked the earl. But he wasn't the gentleman she wanted to be sitting next to, and his attentions only irritated her.

He escorted them to their carriage after the concert and asked if they'd be at Almack's on Wednesday. Aunt Everley responded in the affirmative before Eleanor could deny it, and he took the opportunity to solicit the first dance. Eleanor glanced at her aunt, fully aware that there had been no set plans for the following night. Aunt Everley raised an eyebrow meaningly, and Eleanor accepted Tarrock's request.

"You're not engaged, Eleanor," her aunt cautioned once they were all in the carriage and down the street. "A preference for one gentleman is no excuse to slight another, particularly one of even greater consequence."

Eleanor looked at her hands, folded in her lap, to avoid meeting Aunt Everley's gaze.

"I expect you to dance tomorrow as often as you're asked and be agreeable to everyone."

Eleanor nodded but didn't look up.

Dressing for Almack's was so different from preparing for Seventh Night that Eleanor almost laughed. She didn't particularly care how she looked, and she twisted and pinned her hair haphazardly.

"The patronesses will rescind your voucher if you don't try a *little*," Anne said.

"They'll be delighted to have some new gossip to spread around," Eleanor countered. "My poor fashion sense will be just what they want." She caught her sisters' exchanged glances. "I'm sorry. I'll try."

Anne sighed and spelled Eleanor's hair into place, and Sophie retied the sorry attempt at a bow in her sash.

When the carriage pulled up to Almack's, Eleanor pasted a complacent smile on her face, ready to meet Tarrock. He claimed her hand just before the first dance. She accepted two more partners after he left her with Aunt Everley. After the third set, Eleanor was glad to see Aunt Everley by the refreshments. She took a glass of lemonade from the table, preparing to listen to Aunt Everley's conversation with Lady Jersey.

She'd just taken a sip when a voice beside her said, "Miss Maybury?"

Eleanor choked and sputtered as she turned to Mr. Cole, who looked alarmed.

"Forgive me for startling you, Miss Maybury. Are you all right?"

Eleanor put her hand to her mouth and cringed. "I'm well," she said. "But have you tasted the lemonade?" She was used to lukewarm, weak lemonade, but this was both warm and much too strong, as if someone had intentionally left it out in the sun all day.

Lady Jersey heard her and interrupted her own monologue to respond. "It is dreadful tonight. I intend to find out who is responsible and ensure it never happens again."

Eleanor didn't want anyone to lose their positions over bad lemonade. "It's not—I mean—it *is* too strong and not very cold," she said. "But we can fix it. Could I have two glasses of water, please?" She turned to the servant who stood beside the table.

He bowed and left, returning moments later with the requested water. Lady Jersey had resumed her conversation with Aunt Everley, but Eleanor knew they were both watching her. She frowned at the glasses and thought the spell-word. The water froze to ice. Mr. Cole let out a low whistle. Eleanor smiled at him and picked up the first glass, allowing the warmth of her hands to loosen the ice from the glass. She dumped the ice into the bowl of lemonade with a plop, then did the same with the second glass.

"The ice will cool the lemonade and dilute it as it melts," Eleanor explained.

"Well done," Lady Jersey said. "That's the smartest, most helpful bit of magic I've seen from a young lady these many years."

Eleanor curtsied and turned back to Mr. Cole. "I believe the lemonade interrupted you." She smiled.

He laughed. "I was going to ask you to dance."

"Gladly." Eleanor was eager to escape Lady Jersey, who was talking again to her aunt. Even if she hadn't promised Aunt Everley to dance with whoever asked, she would have agreed to go with Mr. Cole. She knew it was foolish of her, but she couldn't help hoping he might have news of his friend. They had only gone through the first few steps when he mentioned

Mr. Weston. Her heart skipped a beat.

"My friend left town rather suddenly last week," he said. "Do you know why he left?"

"He didn't say anything about it to me," she said. "We had a pleasant drive Monday morning, and then I heard on Wednesday that he was in the country." This was all true, except, perhaps, for the pleasantness of the drive. "Have you heard from him at all?"

"Not a word," he said.

"So you don't know when he'll be back?" *Or if,* she added in her head. Even she heard the wistfulness in her voice.

"I expect he'll be back soon."

He said it with a fierce scowl, and Eleanor had the impression that Mr. Weston might be dragged back to town by his cravat.

She changed the subject, and the rest of the dance passed in easy conversation. When the dance ended, Eleanor discovered that Lady Jersey's favorable impression of her magic had made its way around the room with lightning speed. She received sidelong looks, points and whispers, and dozens more requests to dance. She didn't for a moment think that all the gentlemen of the *ton* suddenly appreciated her magical ability, but she had impressed Lady Jersey, and that was something they took notice of. Countess Lieven nodded approvingly to her, which was more notice than she'd ever received from that quarter, and Princess Esterhazy smiled at her as she passed. Aunt Everley looked pleased as punch. Eleanor rarely even made it to her aunt's side before her next partner claimed her.

Tarrock claimed a second dance with her halfway through the evening. Eleanor stifled a sigh and went with him to the set.

CHAPTER 16

"That was a neat little parlor trick," he said as they danced. "I don't believe anyone has ever done magic at Almack's before. But you've impressed the patronesses, which was a clever move."

Eleanor cringed at his referring again to magic as a parlor trick, as if an elegant lady's display of accomplishments were all magic was good for. "I wasn't trying to impress," she said. "I wanted to fix the lemonade so that it could be drunk, and also to keep whoever made it from getting into trouble."

Tarrock scoffed. "They deserve whatever repercussions are coming their way. The poor quality was deliberate, I'm sure, and if not, then they need to be held to the patronesses' high standards."

Eleanor bit her lip and reaffixed her smile. How could he be so cavalier about someone losing their job over bad lemonade? He was an earl, and as such had been trained by society to think highly of himself, but surely he didn't think that the pleasure of an elite few was worth dismissing everyone else?

It was a relief to finish the dance with him and to know that he couldn't ask her again without risking the censure of the patronesses. Another gentleman asked her immediately, and Eleanor danced without a pause for the rest of the evening, keeping her false smile in place the whole time. She would have been exhausted and footsore if she weren't so very used to dancing.

When the evening ended, Eleanor collapsed in the carriage between her sisters, both of whom had danced nearly every dance as well. They both appeared to be really satisfied with the evening, while Eleanor could only look back with genuine pleasure on her dance with Mr. Cole. She would have been happy to have his friendship as the wife of Mr. Weston. Now, however, it looked as if they couldn't be friends—to avoid Mr. Weston meant avoiding Mr. Cole too.

Aunt Everley sent them all straight to bed upon their arrival at home. Eleanor accepted Sarah's help to get out of her dress, then sent her to Sophie. She locked the door and finally allowed her cheerful facade to crack and crumble. She lay in bed, weak, weary, heartsore, and empty.

Chapter 17

James was frowning at several papers on his desk when George Cole barged in. His friend was agitated, but all James could do was gape at him.

"What are you doing here?" he asked finally. His friend had said nothing about riding out to join him in the country.

"What are *you* doing here?" George demanded. "You left without saying a word."

"I sent you a note."

George gave him a look. "Did she turn you down?"

"I beg your pardon?"

"Miss Eleanor Maybury. Did she reject you?"

James blinked. "No! Why would you think that?"

"You left the ball early on Saturday, you were in a right state on Sunday, and then you disappeared after driving with her on Monday. What am I supposed to think?"

James had to acknowledge that the situation lent itself to such an interpretation. He couldn't explain himself without betraying Eleanor's confidence, however. He shuffled the papers on his desk for a moment to give himself time to think, but he couldn't even remember what was written on them. He hadn't been particularly focused since leaving town. He believed Eleanor—he had decided days ago that her story had been true. But something still kept him away. He'd doubted her, questioned her honor and her honesty, suspected her of untenable behavior. What apology could he make for his own faithlessness? Would she even speak to him again? That question kept him up until nearly dawn each night—he couldn't bear returning to town only for her to wish nothing to do with him.

George was watching him, waiting for an answer.

"I have not made her an offer," James said.

George plunked into the chair opposite the desk. "What the hell are you waiting for?"

"Sorry?" James raised an eyebrow. Cole rarely cursed.

"You have spoken of this girl more often and more admiringly than you have of any other person, ever. And I've known you since Eton. Do you think you're going to find someone you like better?"

"Of course not."

"Then what—" George shook his head and began again. "I saw her at Almack's last night."

James's heart picked up the pace. "How did she look?"

"Pale." George gave him a hard look. "She did magic."

"At Almack's?"

"Right in front of Lady Jersey. The lemonade was overly warm and too strong. She asked for two glasses of water, and without a word, without a touch, she turned them both to ice and added them to the lemonade. *You* couldn't have done it better."

James felt a surge of pride and admiration for Eleanor. "What did Lady Jersey do?"

"Told everyone in the room. Miss Eleanor did not sit out a single dance for the rest of the night. I can tell you firsthand that she danced with a duke, a marquess, an earl, and two baronets, not to mention those of us who haven't come into our titles yet."

James was on his feet and pacing the room before he realized it. His jaw clenched tight.

"Why does this surprise you?" George asked, incredulous. "Tell me what you like about her."

"What?"

"What do you like about her?"

James sighed. "She's sweet, intelligent, sensible, kind, talented, beautiful—"

"And she has fifteen thousand pounds."

James glared at George. "You know that's not—"

"Not something you care about. I know. But other gentlemen find it very appealing. And if you add that sum to all her other charms—can you wonder that she's popular?"

James jammed his hands into his waistcoat pockets and scowled.

George looked away, choosing to study his fingernails. "Tarrock danced with her twice."

Jealousy lurched in James's gut. He had to go back. He couldn't lose her to Tarrock—to any of them. His fingers closed on something in his pocket, and he absently pulled it out. A slip of paper, a scribbled note in a light, fine hand. Eleanor's spell.

James knew exactly what he had to do.

Late on Friday morning, James strode through Portman Square. After working Eleanor's spell, he and Cole had ridden for town, arriving well after dark. Despite the ride and the late hour, James couldn't sleep, and he was on the move early. He had a few other calls to make before he could call on the Mayburys, and the restlessness of the night before continued until he was actually in sight of their house. He was still at the end of the street when he saw three figures walking out the front door and turn toward Hyde Park. James recognized Eleanor immediately, with her sister and John Farrow. He picked up his pace and hailed them. Eleanor froze and reached out to her sister, but Miss Maybury had already paused as well. They waited for him to catch them up. He regretted arriving out of breath, but it was worth it not to miss them.

He bowed. "I was just going to call at your house when I saw you walking out. May I join you?"

Farrow smiled knowingly at Miss Maybury. Eleanor was looking at the cobblestones. Her bonnet was blocking half of her face, but he could see her blush and bite her lip. She nodded but didn't meet his eyes.

They began walking again, Farrow and Miss Maybury in front. James kept his pace purposely slower than theirs, limping a bit more than actually necessary, to allow them to get out of earshot.

When he was sure they couldn't overhear, he steeled himself and said, "I owe you an apology, Miss Eleanor, for doubting you, for entertaining—even for a second—suspicions of which I can't think now without abhorrence. I know it's unforgivable, but I beg your forgiveness anyway."

Eleanor looked up at him, her eyes wide in surprise. "You believe me?"

"Your story was too far-fetched to be false." James felt a weak smile twitching his lips. "If you'd been lying, I'm sure your tale would have been much more plausible."

"And you would have seen through me immediately. I'm a terrible liar." She smiled, but it faded quickly. After a long pause, she asked, "Did you actually have business in the country?"

"No."

"Did you leave town to avoid me?" Her voice shook, and she bit her lip again.

James wished he could tell her anything but the truth. "Yes." He sighed. "As soon as I calmed down, I knew I believed you. I should have come back the very next day. But I was a coward."

Another faint smile. "We both know you're not—"

"But I was. I'm quite serious. I stayed away out of sheer cowardice. I knew I had behaved deplorably toward you, and I was so afraid that I'd forfeited your good opinion. I couldn't bear your rejection."

"So you stayed away. What gave you courage to come back?"

"The thought of you dancing at Almack's with every eligible, young lord in town."

Her smile widened. "I assume Mr. Cole found you?"

"He did. How did you know?"

"Something he said at Almack's suggested that he might."

James wanted to ask what his friend had said, but he refused to get drawn off the subject. He continued, "Now that I've confessed to cowardice and jealousy, in addition to every other reason you should hate me, may I tell you something that might make you think better of me?"

"Nonsense, Mr. Weston. I don't think so ill of you."

"You should."

She looked up at him again. "Should I? After everything, after I even used magic on you, should I blame you for what you thought? That's hardly fair."

Hope swelled in James's heart as it hadn't in nearly two weeks. It was like a balloon lifting him so that his feet barely touched the ground.

"So you don't hate me?"

"Not at all."

He grinned in relief. "May I tell you something anyway?"

"Of course."

"I tried your spell. I used the largest barrel I could get my hands on. This morning I met with a surgeon friend of mine, and we delivered it to St. George's Hospital. I have placed an order with the cooper for half a dozen more barrels, while Dr. Miller makes a list of where to bestow them."

Eleanor turned her sweetest smile on him. "You did?" James thought his insides might melt. "I was sure you would have forgotten about it."

Faced with that smile, James was not about to admit that he had forgotten until he'd found the spell in his pocket. Instead, he offered Eleanor his arm, and his stomach leapt when she took it. "It worked perfectly." He paused. "It was *your* spell, wasn't it? Not your friend's."

Eleanor blushed and nodded. "How could you tell?"

James remembered casting the spell on the barrel. It had been such a simple, effective spell, and if magic could have a smell, this one smelled like wildflowers—like Eleanor. "Just a sense. Have I told you yet how incredible—"

At that moment, the sound of hooves sent them to the side of the path. Rather than continuing on, the rider stopped. James looked up to see the Earl of Tarrock on an imposing bay gelding. Tarrock bowed from his seat and asked Eleanor how she did, and whether she were quite recovered from all the dancing Wednesday night at Almack's. Farrow and Miss Maybury backtracked to join the conversation. After pleasantries about the ball—which Tarrock knew perfectly well that James and Farrow had not attended—the earl took the liberty of requesting a dance at the next ball with Eleanor. James couldn't help himself; he pulled his arm in a little tighter to his side, drawing Eleanor a step closer to him. She smiled and demurred, declaring that Lady Everley was in charge of their schedule, and she wasn't sure what events they would be attending.

"Well, I hope you will honor me whenever we next have the chance," Tarrock said. With another bow, and a dark look at James, he rode away.

A smile played across Miss Maybury's face. "I wonder why he didn't choose to stop and walk with us." She shot Eleanor an amused glance and walked on.

<u>"Because he's not fool enough to try it," James grumbled. Every time he saw Tarrock he thought of three or four spells he'd like to use on him.</u>

Eleanor gave a little giggle-hiccup, as if she'd tried to hold it in but couldn't. James felt a smile pulling at the edge of his scowl at the sound.

Eleanor spoke lightly but quietly enough that only he could hear her. "You know, Lord Tarrock has been very attentive lately." James's jaw clenched, and his arm tightened in to his side even more. Her smile twitched in amusement. "It's a shame that his lack of interest in magic is only matched by my lack of interest in him."

James stopped walking and turned to her. She grinned up at

him. He felt like he was soaring, flying high on the news that Eleanor didn't hate him and she didn't like Tarrock. <u>He could have kissed her right then, in broad daylight, in the middle of Hyde Park, with her sister and everyone else watching. With a great effort, he turned and walked on. He couldn't think of a single thing to say, because all he wanted to do was tell her how much he loved her, and he didn't want an audience for that either.</u>

After a moment, Eleanor said, "I don't know if you've heard, but Anne is engaged to Mr. Farrow. Since last Thursday."

"I'm happy for them." James smiled. "I'm sure they'll do very well together."

They had reached the gate of the park again. Eleanor looked like she'd be willing to walk farther, and James would have walked forever just to keep her close to him, but Miss Maybury professed herself tired and ready to return to the house. They walked back to Portman Square. Pausing in front of the house, James congratulated the newly engaged couple before they went inside. Eleanor was slow to follow, and James hoped that it was reluctance to let go of his arm. He took her hand and pressed it to his lips, enjoying the blush that crept over her cheeks, before she turned and entered the house.

My apologies for the lack of commentary in the last few chapters. I'm just swooning over here, hence all the underlines. I like to joke that my job is playing matchmaker for my imaginary friends, and I love every minute.

Chapter 18

Eleanor was floating on air for the rest of the day. She struggled for composure—she didn't want her joy to be any more obvious than her misery had been—but she knew she was unsuccessful. Anne was the only one who understood and shared in her happiness. To Aunt Everley, Mr. Weston's return was unsurprising, and Eleanor's extreme reactions to his absence and return were unnecessary. Sophie was grave, and only her solemn looks enabled Eleanor to rein in her spirits.

He hasn't even offered, Eleanor told herself sternly, as she caught herself dancing around the room getting dressed the next morning. *He hasn't declared his love or done anything that he hadn't done before he left.*

But he believed me, she thought. *He forgave me and asked me to forgive him. He used the spell I gave him. Isn't that a proof of affection?*

She applied herself to her sewing with new fervor that morning, finishing the embroidery soon after breakfast. She took the silk and her note-filled copy of *Ford's* to her bedroom for some quiet and privacy to work the spell. Eleanor was glad of her sisters' encouragement not to give up and thankful for Lady Snow's advice to finish the spell. Now she cast it, holding the silk in her hands and concentrating hard on the unfamiliar spell-word. It took. She could feel the magic sinking into the silk fibers, infusing them with power. Laughing with relief, she folded the fabric and wrapped it in a handkerchief. She tied it with a ribbon and carried it downstairs, tucking it into her work basket for safekeeping.

Sophie was playing the pianoforte when Eleanor returned to the drawing room, a loud, forceful song without words. Eleanor sighed. Her sister's moods could be guessed by how she played and what songs she chose. She wished Sophie could be happy, or at least less miserable. When Sophie finished playing, Eleanor suggested walking out to call on friends. Sophie agreed readily, always preferring to be outdoors and in motion.

They didn't talk as they walked. There was nothing to say, and a footman was walking only a few steps behind. But Eleanor hoped that maybe it helped to have time just for the two of them to be together as sisters.

They returned from their social call in time to have tea and dress for yet another ball that night. Eleanor hadn't thought she could ever tire of dancing—she'd eagerly attended a ball every week for the past five years—but London Society was beginning to wear on her. If Mr. Weston was there, however, she could at least look forward to a pleasant dance or two.

Eleanor was climbing the stairs to her room to dress for the ball when Papa arrived home. He'd been out for most of the day, between business and the club, like most days this Season. As he handed his coat, hat, and gloves to Harvey, he asked if anyone had called for him.

"A Mr. Weston, sir. He left his card and said he'd call again at your earliest convenience."

They moved away so that Eleanor couldn't hear her father's response, but she'd heard enough to set her heart pounding. Nobody had mentioned Mr. Weston's call to Eleanor when she'd come home. Had he called specifically to speak to Papa?

She flitted up the rest of the stairs to her room. Several deep breaths calmed her enough to choose a dress so that she was ready when Anne came in. They helped each other into their gowns and braided each other's hair and then went to look for Sophie. Sophie was seated in front of the mirror in her room, frowning at her hairbrush as if deep in thought. She didn't appear to hear them open the door. She started and looked up when Anne asked if she needed help with her hair.

"Yes, please," Sophie said simply.

Eleanor frowned. Sophie was never so subdued and distracted.

When all three were ready, they went down to the carriage. Sophie remained preoccupied for the ride across town. Eleanor was uneasy, but as she had no specific concerns to raise, she kept her worries to herself. Her own attention was called away as soon as they entered the ballroom by Mr. Weston, who appeared at her side, as solemn as ever.

"Save all your waltzes for me," he murmured.

"And what if there are more than two?"

"Then I shall scandalize the *ton* by dancing with you for half the evening." His mouth quirked.

"You wouldn't."

"Try me." The corners of his mouth turned up a bit more. "I'm afraid that if you dance in another gentleman's arms, you may find them spellbound, and not in a good way."

Eleanor giggled. "You *wouldn't*."

"I might." He flashed her a quick, brilliant smile and

disappeared into the gathered crowd.

See? Swoon. <3

The dancing began. Eleanor enjoyed herself much more than she was expecting, though she'd seen the same people at the same gatherings for weeks and weeks now. Anne was smiling and laughing, and it warmed Eleanor to see her sister so happy. Sophie was smiling too and dancing every dance. Eleanor told herself she'd been reading too much into Sophie's mood earlier.

And nothing could worry her when Mr. Weston came to claim the first waltz. His hand on the small of her back was strong and warm, and she wondered what it would feel like to throw her arms around his neck and let him hold her close.

During their second waltz, the air seemed to fizzle around them. Mr. Weston was smiling, and Eleanor thought, once or twice, that he was on the verge of saying something, but he didn't. She didn't speak either—she couldn't seem to catch her breath.

Lord Tarrock asked her for a dance soon afterward. Eleanor couldn't forget Mr. Weston's reaction to the lord's presence yesterday, but as he hadn't yet made her an offer, she couldn't refuse Tarrock a dance. The earl seemed preoccupied as they danced, lapsing into absentminded silence at odd times. When the dance finished, he procured punch and led her to a corner where they could be out of the way. Eleanor sipped her punch, grateful for the cool liquid and the fact that it was quite good without magical help. She kept darting glances at Tarrock as she drank. He didn't seem to want to leave her side, but he wasn't talking either. At length, Eleanor finished her drink, and Tarrock, blinking at her as if he'd dragged his mind back from a long way away, downed the rest of his glass. He took her empty glass and set them both on a side table, then he turned to face her directly.

"Miss Eleanor, I believe my attentions have been too marked to be misunderstood. I've admired you since the moment we met. It would make me the happiest man in the world if you would consent to be my wife. There's... there's something special about you, and I'd like to spend the rest of my life figuring it out."

Eleanor gaped at him. Not because he was proposing—he was right, his attentions had been easy to comprehend—but because of his last statement. She shook her head. "I don't know how special I truly am, but whatever it is, you could have figured it out by now if you'd tried."

Lord Tarrock colored. "I beg your pardon?"

"You've never once asked me about myself. What is my favorite flower? What is my favorite color?"

"White...?" He guessed weakly, glancing down at her dress.

Eleanor raised an eyebrow. All the young ladies in the *ton* preferred white, if their ball gowns were going to be the standard of judgement. "How do I spend the majority of my time?"

He blinked at her. "In morning calls and parties and walking in the park, like everyone else."

Eleanor shook her head again. "But what about the rest of

my time?"

A smile began to pull at the corners of his mouth. "Getting ready to do it all again. Is this a trick question?"

"But, see, that's it—that's why I can't accept you. You haven't taken the time to get to know me at all."

His smile disappeared, replaced by a scowl. "And Weston has?"

Eleanor stared at him.

"Don't take me for a fool, Miss Eleanor. I've seen the way you look at him. If you had ever looked at me like that—even once—we'd have been before the archbishop by now." He looked away, and Eleanor could see the tight line of his clenched jaw. He took a deep breath and turned back. "I'm not one to concede defeat so easily. I'm an earl, for goodness' sake, and what is he? An untitled upstart with a handful of magic tricks!"

At this, Eleanor turned to walk away. She'd made her case; she didn't need to stand there listening to him abuse Mr. Weston and magic in general.

He caught her arm, tugging a bit harder than was necessary to turn her to face him. She opened her mouth to demand he let her go, but before she could get the words out, he dropped her arm and stared at his hand. His palm was as red as if he'd been scalded.

"If you ever lay a hand on her again, I promise to use spells that are both more painful and more permanent." Mr. Weston's voice was low but icy as he stalked toward them.

Tarrock glared at him. "You wouldn't dare."

"It's not in your best interest to test me," Mr. Weston said, his glower darker than Eleanor had ever seen it. "I suggest you leave."

CHAPTER 18

Tarrock clearly had no intention of complying. He stood his ground, and Eleanor worried that this would turn into a scene, here in a crowded ballroom of all places. Suddenly Sophie appeared at her side, hooking her arm through Eleanor's and looking back and forth between the two men. Her innocent confusion seemed to bring Tarrock to his senses. He unclenched his fists, turned on his heel, and stormed away.

Eleanor took a shaky breath, realizing she'd been holding it ever since Mr. Weston had joined them.

"Are you all right?" Sophie whispered.

Eleanor nodded.

"Are you ready?"

Eleanor nodded again. "I just need a minute."

Sophie let go of her arm and stepped a few paces away. Eleanor turned to Mr. Weston, whose expression softened as soon as he looked at her.

"Are you hurt?"

"No," she said. "Thank you."

He dropped his head in a slight bow. He glanced at Sophie. "You're going?"

Eleanor nodded. "I don't know how many we have left. I can't take this from Sophie."

He took her hand and brushed a kiss over her knuckles. "I'll look for you when you come back."

Eleanor turned and took Sophie's hand, then thought the spell-word to make them unnoticeable. She felt Mr. Weston's eyes on them, even after the spell took hold.

They found a small sitting room with a side door. Eleanor locked the door and opened the gate, while Sophie circled the room. They crept down the marble staircase together. Sophie seemed preoccupied again, but Eleanor wasn't surprised—this was their first Seventh Night without Anne. Everything else remained the same, however, and they joined the dance.

When the dancing ended, Lady Snow spoke to Eleanor for a moment about the spell, commending her on having finished it. "Remember what I've taught you," she said. "And once you have ceased to be a child, you might still find me at times. When a full moon shines on Midwinter's Eve; when it snows on the first day of spring; then walk into a meadow and look for me."

Eleanor hardly knew what to say. She thanked the Fae lady for her friendship and teaching and promised to remember her words. Tears pricked at her eyes.

She turned to look for Sophie, who was talking earnestly with Lord River. Eleanor approached them, ready to return home. They fell silent as she drew close, and Lord River turned his silvery eyes on her.

"It is nearly your time, child," he said. "You may only come back once more, and then the gate will no longer open for you."

Eleanor bit her lip and nodded. She turned to Sophie. "Are you ready?"

Sophie drew a deep breath. "I'm not going."

Eleanor blinked at her. "What do you mean?"

"I'm not going back. If Her Majesty agrees, I'm staying here." Sophie began to walk toward the colonnade where the Queen still sat.

"But—you can't! You don't live here, you live at home with us!"

"And you and Anne are getting married and moving away," Sophie said. "I have nothing left there."

"What about Papa?"

"He'll understand."

"No," Eleanor argued. "He won't. And you don't have to stay with Papa or Aunt Everley after Anne and I leave—you can stay with one of us."

Sophie made a face. "Because I want to stay with the newlyweds."

"At least we'd be together."

"But don't you see, Eleanor? I love it here. I've always loved Faerie more than home—it was only you and Anne that kept me from staying ages ago."

Eleanor swallowed back a lump in her throat. "You can come back, though. It's not your last time."

Sophie shook her head. "I can't hold more than two spells at a time by myself, and I can't leave from London without all of them. I'd have to wait months until I'm back at Fairfield to sneak away."

Eleanor was suddenly struck by the silver that laced the blue of her sister's eyes. How had she not noticed it before? Or was it just that her own eyes were filling with tears?

"You can't stay—not yet. Not without saying goodbye to Anne. Come back tonight, and you can stay next week."

"If I go home, I'm afraid you won't let me come back. You won't open the gate, or Anne will talk me out of it somehow. Please," Sophie pleaded. "Please give my love to Anne—and to Charles and Henry, if you can find a way—but I have to stay now."

"Sophie..." Eleanor's mind was a roaring blank of helplessness. She couldn't leave her sister behind. She just couldn't.

Sophie took her hand, squeezed it, and slipped through the crowd around the Queen.

Eleanor looked around for someone to help, someone to take

her side, but Lord River was standing before Her Majesty with Sophie, and Lady Snow was nowhere to be seen. Panicking, Eleanor fled through the passage and up the stairs, running as fast as she could in her gown and slippers. She'd find Anne. Anne could surely convince Sophie. And if she couldn't, at least she could say goodbye.

Eleanor gasped out a sob at the thought. No. They couldn't lose Sophie.

She pelted through the gate and stumbled against a chair in the sitting room. She closed the gate, because that was the first rule Lord River had taught them—never leave the gate open. She unlocked the door and pushed her way into the ballroom, getting close to Anne before she let down the unnoticeable spell.

"What's the matter?" Anne said when she saw her, her smile fading.

"I need your help," Eleanor gasped. "We have to go back—"

"I can't," Anne hissed. "I'm not allowed."

"But I need you! It's about So—"

"I told you, I can't go through the gate," Anne said. "If you need to go back, I can work the old time spell for you, the one we used before you learned the chronology spell. I can give you an hour. But people are looking at you, so you'd better go now."

Eleanor opened her mouth to protest. She hadn't expected Anne to refuse to come. She turned to leave the ballroom again, trying desperately to come up with a new plan.

Chapter 19

James had stood at the side of the ballroom for the last ten minutes, leaning against the wall and pretending not to wait for Eleanor. He sensed when her main spells ended. He stood up straight and turned his attention to the door. A moment later, she entered alone and went straight to her sister. She looked agitated. He began making his way toward her. He didn't know what was wrong, but she was upset about something.

She turned away from Anne. He hurried between people and caught up with her at the door.

"Miss Maybury," he began. She whirled, and her frown relaxed into a relieved smile. James forgot what he was about to say.

"Mr. Weston, will you help me?"

"Of course," he said quickly. "What is the matter?"

"We have to go back," Eleanor said, turning and leading the way out of the ballroom. "Anne's going to do a time spell for us, but she can only give us an hour, so we have to hurry."

"An hour to do what?" James asked. He could think of several things he'd like to do with Eleanor for an hour, but he'd have to marry her first.

Eleanor didn't seem to hear him. "I don't know how to convince her…." She opened the door to a sitting room and strode across the room to another door. She paused and looked back at him. "Can you please lock that one?"

James closed the door and used a locking spell, then turned back to Eleanor, frowning. "What are we doing?"

"We have to stop her from eating anything." She was frowning at the door in front of her. When she turned the handle, a marble staircase that could not possibly have fit in this house descended away from her. She glanced back at James, urgency and agitation in every move. "Come on, quickly, and shut the door behind you." She started down the stairs.

James hurried after her, getting more and more worried. "What are we doing? I assume we're going to Faerie, but why do you need my help?"

"We can't just leave her," she said, more to herself than to him. "She doesn't know what she's talking about."

"Eleanor!" James burst. "What is going on?"

Eleanor stopped suddenly as if she'd run into a wall. She turned to him, her face unreadable. He realized a second too late that he'd used only her Christian name.

"Forgive me, Miss Maybury, but how am I to help you if I don't know what the problem is?"

"No, I'm sorry, I should have explained," she said softly. "It's Sophie. She wouldn't come back with me."

James stared at her, horrified. "She stayed behind in Faerie?"

Eleanor nodded. "And if she eats Fae food, she'll be there forever, so we have to get to her before she does. I don't know how to convince her to come back. I was hoping Anne would come with me to talk to her, but Anne wouldn't—can't—come."

"What can I do to help?"

"I don't know," she shrugged helplessly, hurrying down the

stairs again. "I just thought having another magician with me would be a good idea."

James thought that the two of them would be vastly outmatched if it came to a magical contest with the Fae, but he kept that to himself.

<u>It seemed like a foolhardy idea, the two of them charging into Faerie without the smallest plan, but James was prepared to go to the ends of the earth and beyond with Eleanor.</u> He'd been in tighter spots with the Royal Navy, and a plan had always presented itself. So he rushed down the stairs and along a matching corridor, ignoring the stiffness in his leg that always followed dancing. He'd be limping badly tomorrow, but he'd deal with that when the time came.

At last, the corridor emptied onto a wide, flat colonnade. James gasped. The sky above the colonnade was a blue so intense a person could drown in it. The marble glowed in the dusky golden sunlight, though they'd left the ball an hour before midnight. Eleanor didn't seem to notice the view. She strode off across the colonnade, and James trotted to keep up.

A tall figure materialized in front of them. The gentleman was dressed with perfect, simple elegance, his complexion flawless, his long dark hair tied back from his face. But it was his eyes—his silver-gray, waterfall eyes—that told James without question that this was the Faerie that Eleanor called Lord River, her grandfather.

Eleanor came to a halt. "Where's Sophie?" she demanded.

The tall gentleman half turned and gestured to the meadow beyond the stretch of marble. Sophie sat at the edge of the grass, sharing a bowl of grapes with a tall, icy, Fae lady. Eleanor's face fell. Sophie had eaten Fae food.

"How could you let her do this?" Her accusation only made

Lord River raise a perfectly curved brow.

"It was her choice," he said calmly. "She is of age. But you, child—you've brought a mortal to our realm, which I specifically forbade."

"To help me rescue Sophie."

"Rescue? She doesn't appear to need rescuing to me." Lord River studied Eleanor for a moment. "You know what becomes of mortals in Faerie."

Any mortal in Faerie must stay for a year and a day—no more, no less—regardless of whether they eat the food. That rule doesn't apply to the Maybury sisters, since they have fae blood. They can come and go every Seventh Night, but eating fae food will keep them there forever. Both are versions of traditional mythology, which has plenty of variations to play with.

"Not if he's with me." She scowled fiercely.

Lord River laughed. "Setting that aside, what were you planning to do? Your attempts to reason with your sister have already failed. Two human magicians are hardly a match for the whole of Faerie, if you were hoping to take her by magic. Or were you intending to sling her over your shoulder and carry her off by force?"

Eleanor glared at him but said nothing.

"You used up your last visit, and for what?" The Faerie's

tone was cool, but James thought he cared more than he let on. "I told you the gate would only open for you once more, and you've opened it."

"I couldn't just leave her here alone." Eleanor's voice came out very small. Her eyes darted to the woods on the far side of the meadow.

"She's safe with me, child," Lord River said gently. "I will take care of her."

"Yes, but..."

"Her Majesty has already accepted your sister's request to stay. The only way you could take her away now is by leaving someone in trade. Would you stay behind to send her home? Or would you leave your friend?"

The Fae gentleman's eyes turned to James, who found himself unable to move beneath the silvery gaze. Eleanor took two steps closer to James and grabbed his hand in hers, holding it fiercely, protectively, while glaring again at her grandfather. James breathed easier as Lord River looked at Eleanor with an amused smirk. He clasped her hand tightly in his.

"It looks to me like you need to accept your sister's decision," Lord River said.

"But how could you let her choose this?" Eleanor asked again.

"Child," the Faerie said with surprising kindness. "You and your elder sister have chosen the life that will make you happy. Why should your younger sister not be allowed to do the same?"

Eleanor sighed, almost a sob. "But I'll never see her again."

"Even changes for the better can be difficult, child." Lord River stepped closer to them and cupped Eleanor's face in his hands. James's grip on her hand tightened further. The Faerie bent forward and pressed his lips against Eleanor's forehead. "And though you don't need it, you have my blessing."

He stepped back and began to fade. James looked around and discovered that it wasn't just Lord River who was fading: all of Faerie was fading to gray, and what materialized around them was a lavish sitting room in a London house. Eleanor let go of James's hand and whirled to the door that had once been a Faerie gate. She opened it, revealing only another dark, ordinary room. She closed the door again with a soft click and stood with her head bowed.

The latch snicked with such finality that it stole Eleanor's breath. She'd never see Sophie again. She'd never walk the passage to Faerie again. She'd never see Lord River or Her Majesty or Lords Storm and Orion.

The ridiculousness of rushing back to Faerie hit her fully. What had she expected to happen? If she'd only waited, she could go back next week and see her sister one more time.

Mr. Weston's gentle voice came from close behind her. "Miss Maybury."

Eleanor turned, and in one step closed the distance between them. She rested her head against Mr. Weston's chest and wept, her tears soaking his coat. His arms came around her, and he held her, patient and quiet while she cried. When her tears had subsided into wet hiccups, he let go with one arm to draw a handkerchief from his pocket for her before enfolding her in both arms again. Eleanor took a deep, shuddering breath and sighed. After everything, Mr. Weston's arms were comforting and safe, and she'd gladly stay there for hours.

Mr. Weston rested his cheek against the top of her head. "My sweet Eleanor, I love you," he murmured, "but I'll wait another fortnight to offer for you if it means you can go see your sister again."

Eleanor's heart warmed at his generosity, but she gave her head a tiny shake. "I can't go back. The gate won't open for me again. Sophie made her choice, and now I have to live with it."

Mr. Weston pulled back just a little so he could look her in the eye. "Then will you marry me?"

"Of course I will," Eleanor said. He pulled her close again and kissed the top of her head. "Did you actually think I wouldn't?"

"No," he said. Then, in a lighter tone, "Especially not after you took my hand so possessively back there. I do appreciate your unwillingness to leave me behind."

Eleanor smiled. "It seemed a shame to never hear you call me Eleanor again."

"Eleanor..." he said softly.

She looked up, thinking he might kiss her and perfectly willing for that to happen. Instead, he stepped back and let her go, as though with a vast amount of effort.

"We should get you back to the ballroom. I'm sure we've used up our whole hour." His voice was gruff.

Eleanor was sure her face was a blotchy, tear-stained mess. "I can't go back looking like this."

"Nonsense," Mr. Weston said. He took the handkerchief from her hand, frowned at it, and then gently wiped her face. The cloth was unexpectedly damp, cool, and refreshing. "You look beautiful."

"Mr. Weston—" Eleanor began.

"Call me James?"

"James—"

The sunlight warmth of his smile dazzled her. She forgot everything in that moment.

"I like the sound of that," he said. "What did you want to ask me?"

"I don't remember," she said weakly.

Mr. Weston—James—chuckled. He took her hand and kissed it, then tucked her arm through his.

Eleanor shook her head to clear it. "But your coat..."

James looked down at the tear-soaked patch on the front of his coat. He ran his hand slowly down over it. It was instantly dry and clean, as though fresh from the laundress.

"You have *got* to teach me that spell."

James chuckled again. "Every spell I know."

James knew they needed to slip unnoticed into the ballroom, but it was hard to feel secretive with Eleanor on his arm and his offer accepted. Fortunately, the room was crowded enough that no one paid them much attention.

Until they reached Eleanor's aunt.

Lady Everley gasped and flushed at the sight of them. "Where have you been?" she hissed at Eleanor. "I've been looking for you for the past quarter hour. And where is Sophie?"

CHAPTER 19

Eleanor blanched. James realized instantly that she'd forgotten to use the spell to go unnoticed when they'd gone back to Faerie.

"Sophie and I went... to the necessary," Eleanor stammered, her face going suddenly bright red. "And then..."

She really was a terrible liar, James thought. "And then I met them on my way to the card room," he cut in smoothly. "Miss Sophie was good enough to give us a moment of privacy. I couldn't wait another minute to declare my feelings, and Eleanor has been gracious enough to accept me." He glanced sideways at her. She was still blushing, but she was obviously trying—unsuccessfully—not to smile. "Sir William was out when I called this morning, but I intend to call again at his earliest convenience."

Lady Everley blinked at them. "Well, that's... I mean... that's very..." She took a steadying breath. "I wish you very happy, of course. But where is Sophie?"

"She isn't here?" Eleanor squeaked.

James bit back a laugh. He didn't want her to learn to lie, but she really was dreadful at it.

"She's not dancing," Lady Everley said, apparently oblivious to Eleanor's discomfort. "And I can't see her among the wallflowers either."

"We'd best look for her, then," James said. "Eleanor, why don't you and Miss Maybury check every corner of the ballroom? I'll check the terrace. Perhaps Lady Everley will look in the card room?"

Miss Maybury had joined them, and she agreed readily. Eleanor walked off arm in arm with her sister. James was sure Eleanor would whisper the truth to Anne as soon as they were out of earshot. To be convincing, James pressed through the crowd toward the open terrace. He didn't know what Lady Everley and Sir William would think about Sophie's disappearance, but he didn't envy their worry.

Chapter 20

Eleanor stared absently out the sitting room window. She was alone, so there was no point pretending to be occupied. In fact, everyone in the house was too distracted to expect otherwise. She heard the door open behind her and turned, thinking it was her sister or her aunt.

Mr. Weston stepped into the room. <u>Without stopping to think, Eleanor ran to him. His strong arms came around her, and she relaxed for the first time since they'd returned to the ballroom last night.</u> After a moment but much too soon, she let go and stepped back.

"What are you doing here?" she asked. "I'm hardly dressed for company." She looked down at her dress, a light blue faded even paler with age.

Mr. Weston reached out a gentle hand and lifted her chin. "You look wonderful." He leaned down and kissed her, softly and exquisitely. Eleanor shivered. He pulled back and smiled.

"But what are you doing here?" she breathed. "They don't let in visitors on Sunday."

"Your father asked me to call on him this morning, and he suggested that I might find you here."

"You've spoken to him?"

James nodded. "The banns will be published immediately."

Banns are an engagement announcement read aloud in church. They are read in the home parish of each member of the couple and in the church where the wedding will take place. They must be read three times with no one contesting the match before the wedding can happen. This is still a tradition in the Church of England.

Eleanor wanted to kiss him again, but she knew Anne and Aunt Everley could arrive any minute. He must have been thinking the same thing, because he asked, "Why are you alone this morning?"

"Anne and our aunt are finishing breakfast. I wasn't hungry." As she spoke, Eleanor crossed to a chair by the table. She sat and bent over her work basket. Mr. Weston limped over and pulled another chair beside her. Straightening up, Eleanor held out a parcel wrapped in a handkerchief.

"I didn't know if or when I'd be able to give this to you, but it might be useful after last night."

He smiled, puzzled, and unwrapped it. He stared at the green silk as if mesmerized, his eyes fixed on the embroidered violets along the edge.

His silence made Eleanor uncomfortable, so she babbled, "It's a new spell, and I'm not entirely sure it will work. The ones Lady Snow helps me with usually do, though. It's supposed to take away pain and stiffness. It will work best if it's directly against the skin, but it should still work with fabric between."

She trailed off. Mr. Weston was running the silk through his fingers. He met her eyes.

"This is incredible."

Eleanor blushed as he wrapped the silk around his knee.

"I have something for you too," he said, reaching into his pocket. "All the family jewelry will be yours, of course, but I thought you might like this." He held out a ring: two amethysts on either side of a large, oval diamond. "The purple reminded me of your violets," he said shyly. Eleanor gaped at it, speechless. She'd forgotten about betrothal rings and would never have expected one so simple and perfect. "I—I took the liberty of altering it for you." James turned the ring to show her the symbols engraved inside the gold band.

"What do they mean?" Eleanor asked.

"They amplify your magic," he said, a smile playing hopefully at the corners of his mouth. "They also make it easier to work spells together, if the other person has the match." He gestured to the engraved gold band on the second finger of his right hand. "I'll teach you how to use it. May I?" He took her left hand in both of his and slipped the ring onto her finger. They stayed there for an endless moment, their hands entwined.

He gets her. <3

The door opened, and they both started. Anne entered first, pausing as she did to say something over her shoulder to Aunt Everley. That tactful delay gave Mr. Weston a second to jump to his feet and whip the green silk from his leg and tuck it into his pocket. Aunt Everley entered next, and he strode gracefully across the room to bow over her hand and beg forgiveness for his intrusion. Eleanor was pleased to notice that his limp was all but gone. Papa entered the room after his sister. He surveyed Mr. Weston with a small smile before turning to Eleanor.

"Eleanor, may I have a word in the library, please?"

She rose and followed him out of the room with one parting smile at James.

In the library, her father sat at the table where a breakfast tray sat untouched. He poured tea and gestured for Eleanor to join him.

"You didn't sleep last night, I'm guessing," he said.

"No."

"Nor did you eat this morning?"

Eleanor shook her head and sat in the chair beside him.

"Nor did I," Papa said. "But you ought to at least have some tea and toast. We both will."

Eleanor accepted her tea but didn't drink. Papa took a long, slow sip and changed the subject.

"Weston was limping rather badly when he called on me this morning."

"An old war wound," Eleanor said.

Papa nodded. "But when he greeted your aunt just now

there was not even a hint of a limp." He raised an eyebrow at Eleanor, who decided it was a good time to start on her tea. "I did notice," Papa continued, "a silk scarf vanishing into his pocket, with some strikingly familiar embroidery." Eleanor blushed and took another sip of tea. When she finally met his eyes, her father was smiling. "Your mother's gift for magic went far beyond the usual accomplishments. You are so like her, Eleanor, and I'm proud of you. I wish you very happy, and I'm sure you will be."

Eleanor reached out and squeezed her father's hand. Papa hadn't talked about their mother much in the years since her passing. He had loved Mama dearly, and Eleanor was sure he still missed her daily, just like Eleanor did.

They sipped their tea in silence for a moment. Papa set down his cup first. "I wanted to talk to you about Sophie," he said. "I have men searching London top to bottom, and your aunt will be making inquiries of all the ladies who have an ear for gossip. But you saw Sophie last—did she give you any idea of where she was going?"

Eleanor frowned at her teacup. This was the question that had kept her up last night—should she tell? She could spare Papa weeks of worry and trouble if she confessed to the whole truth. But Mama had not told him, and it was Mama's secret as much as anyone's.

She took a deep breath and let it out in a sigh. Mama was gone, and Eleanor and Anne were barred from Faerie. Sophie was missing. Telling now could only help.

"I know where she is," Eleanor said softly. "But it's a long story and a most particular secret. I have to tell it all from the beginning so that you'll understand."

Papa nodded and sat back.

Eleanor told him everything, from Grandmother's deathbed confession to sneaking out every Seventh Night to Sophie's refusal to return with her. "I tried to convince her to come back with me," she whispered. "I went back a second time, but it was too late."

Papa regarded her silently for a long, long time. "Sophie is in Faerie," he said slowly. Eleanor nodded. "With her... grandfather." Eleanor nodded again. "She is safe? Happy?"

Eleanor nodded a third time. "I believe so, Papa."

Papa sighed. "And your mother knew all this and told you about it."

"I'm sorry, Papa."

He shook his head. "Don't be. I knew there was something special about her, but I was so besotted that it never occurred to me to ask what it was." He paused. "And Weston knows?"

"He and Anne are the only others who do."

Papa nodded. "He's a good man, Eleanor." He gazed thoughtfully at the empty teacup in his hand.

"If..." Eleanor began, unsure how to ask her question. "Would you still have married Mama, if you'd known?"

Papa smiled reminiscently. "Nothing could have stopped me from marrying your mother." He paused. "But I'm glad I didn't know. I'm not sure I could have looked your grandfather Kerring in the eye." He ran a hand through his hair. "Eleanor, what am I to tell your brothers? Or Lord Linfield?"

An idea had come to Eleanor in the silent hours of the night. She'd considered acting on it without telling Papa, but she was glad she hadn't. She'd rather explain it to him first. "Need we tell them anything? The spell I've been using to make us unnoticeable when we disappear to Faerie could probably, with a little alteration, be cast on Sophie from afar. She would vanish from the consciousness of anyone who wasn't especially close to her."

"But if Lord Linfield was prepared to propose…"

"Was he, though? He admired Sophie a great deal, but I don't think his affections were so much entangled that the spell would fail to work on him."

"And your brothers?"

Eleanor frowned. "I don't know if it would affect them, and I'm not sure if I'd want it to. It would be easier not to have to make up some story about Sophie going to stay with friends in Scotland or some other distant place, but for her own brothers to forget her—that seems almost cruel."

This was one of the harder chapters to write because of figuring out how to tie up loose ends and deal with an absent Sophie. I wanted her to be able to disappear almost completely, but I didn't want her family to forget her.

Papa nodded. "You work on that spell; I'll come up with the details of the story you suggested for anyone who remembers and asks."

Eleanor got to her feet. "Papa," she said, setting down her half-full teacup. "Do you think Mr. Smith would bring the boys to town for the weddings? I know Anne would like them to be there."

Papa smiled. "I'll send him a note today."

Eleanor thanked him and left the room. She walked to the stairs slowly. She thought Mama would be proud of her courage. Lord River would be proud that she'd told the truth. And Sophie would be glad that Papa wasn't suffering unduly from her choice to stay away. Eleanor took a deep breath, confident that she'd done right and glad that the confession was over.

She took the stairs two at a time, now eager to get back to James. She could use his help altering the spell, and a few more kisses wouldn't go awry. If only her aunt would give them another few minutes alone…

Epilogue

This is not the only epilogue—there are mini epilogues for both Eleanor and Anne in the bonus content available to newsletter subscribers.

Ten years later

"The children are all in bed," Eleanor told her husband, poking her head into his study. "Mrs. Campbell is sitting up with them in case Marianne or Thomas wake."

James looked up at her. "You're really going, then?"

"Of course I am." Eleanor stepped into the room and closed the door. "This is the first full moon on a Midwinter's Eve in years, and I can't miss this chance. Lady Snow may be able to tell me about Sophie."

James got to his feet. "I'm coming with you."

Eleanor frowned at him. "I don't know if she'll meet me if you're there."

"It's much too late, dark, and cold for me to allow my wife

to go out alone," he said firmly. "I'll keep my distance when we get there. Wherever there is."

"She said something about a meadow," Eleanor shrugged. "I was thinking the picnic spot by the stream."

James nodded. "Let's go, then."

They walked together to the entrance hall. Servants brought their coats, along with mittens, warm hats, and extra shawls. They bundled up—winter chill had already settled over most of England. James took a lantern, lit it with a silent spell, and they walked out together.

It was nice, Eleanor thought. They hadn't gone on a moonlight walk together since before Thomas was born. Their older two boys—James and William—had always been good sleepers, and there had been occasional nights the young parents had snuck out while Mrs. Campbell watched over the boys. Thomas had been colicky, and <u>Marianne had simply decided as a baby that she'd rather be awake and exploring than doing anything as dull as sleeping</u>.

I fell in love with Eleanor and James's children too, even though they don't get more than a mention. Marianne is my favorite little spitfire.

James held out his free arm, and Eleanor took it, remembering the time in Hyde Park when she'd held his arm and he'd tugged her a step closer. His jealousy of the Earl of Tarrock had been unfounded but sweet. She smiled up at her husband. He smiled back.

"I saw you got a letter from Charles today," he said after a while. "What did he have to say?"

Eleanor laughed. "My poor brother! Aunt Everley is trying to convince him to go to town this Season so that she can match him with some young heiress."

James shook his head. "Poor man! Do you think he'll go?"

Eleanor shrugged. "He seems to be trying to copy Anne—you know she wouldn't come to town for her Season until we girls were all old enough to go together. He's trying to delay until Henry goes too."

"But Henry came of age last year."

Eleanor nodded. "Which means that now Aunt Everley will start working on Henry as well. But, really, Charles is five-and-twenty years old, and he's already Lord Everley. He won't have any shortage of interested ladies, no matter when he chooses to look."

"Would it help to invite him to visit us instead? The children always love seeing him."

"Oh, let's! What a wonderful idea, and as William and Thomas both have spring birthdays, Aunt Everley won't be able to fault him for coming to us then."

They talked over these plans as they walked. The picnic meadow wasn't far, and they soon reached it. James stopped at the edge of the trees. He set the lantern at his feet and leaned against a tree trunk, watching Eleanor walk into the open.

<u>The grasses were dry and brown and crackling underfoot, laced with moon shadows. Everything looked silvered and Fae. It was nothing like Faerie itself, but it looked like that realm had touched this, breathed a little magic into the</u>

mundane.

"Greetings, child."

Eleanor looked around. She hadn't heard any footsteps but her own. Lady Snow glowed in the moonlight. Her hair, skin, and gown were all as white as the snow that threatened to fall any day now. Her eyes, the blue of snow-shadows, looked as pale silver-gray tonight as Eleanor's own.

Eleanor realized she was holding her breath, and she sighed. "Lady Snow."

"Lord River sends greetings."

Eleanor nodded her thanks. "And Sophie?" she asked wistfully.

"She is well and happy," the lady said. "As it appears you are too."

"You've watched?"

"Of course, child. Your grandfather keeps an eye on all his family." She smiled. "You have used your magic well."

Pride swelled in Eleanor. She had always valued Lady Snow's opinion. But she knew, even without having heard the Faerie say it, that she had done well. She and James together had done much to improve the living conditions of the poor and sick and overworked. Water-cleansing barrels were now in all English hospitals and poorhouses, and James's medical spells were used by half the surgeons in the kingdom. Eleanor had even begun compiling a book of practical spells so that a lady's magical education was worth more than elegance and illusion.

"This visit cannot be long," Lady Snow said. "Nor can I come again soon. I have come as often as I have to set your mind at ease about your sister."

Eleanor remembered something Mama had said a long time ago: "There are only certain times when Fae can enter our world, and even fewer when adults can see them." This was true—she wouldn't call Lady Snow's visits "often" by any means. In the ten years since the gate had closed behind her for the last time, she'd seen the Faerie only thrice, twice during spring snows and then tonight.

"Thank you," Eleanor said. "It helps to hear word of Sophie whenever I can."

Lady Snow nodded once. "Be at ease that she chose well for herself. You will not hear from me for some time. <u>Your children may see us, however.</u>" She gave Eleanor a significant look. "<u>Your daughter has your eyes.</u>"

And then she was gone, fading into the moonlight and leaving only an afterglow that dazzled Eleanor. As her vision adjusted back to the light of the winter moon, she turned to where she'd left James. He was standing a few yards into the meadow, lantern in hand. Eleanor ran to him, and he pulled her close and held her. Silently, he let her go, and they began the walk home.

"What did she say?" James asked.

"Sophie is well and happy."

He frowned down at her. "You ought to be relieved. What else did she say?"

"Lord River will come for Marianne when she's old enough to attend Seventh Night."

James nodded, his expression relaxing. "We expected as much. It's too bad we don't have more girls."

"I think he'll come for Emma and Lucy too," she said, "so she won't be going alone."

Anne's daughters were eight and six, and they doted on their younger cousin. Marianne loved them, but it didn't take long playing dolls and tea indoors before she was speeding outside to join the boys in their games.

It was a shame that Andrea wouldn't be able to go with them, since she had no Faerie blood, but Eleanor supposed that by the time they were old enough, Andrea would be making her debut in town, so she would be too busy to feel left out.

Their three boys could pass the gate into Faerie, but they'd be away at school by the time Marianne was old enough to attend the Seventh Night balls. Perhaps when they were home on holidays their sister could take them along. Eleanor sighed. "At least one of our children will get to meet Sophie."

"And," James said lightly, "when she's old enough for a Season, we need have no concerns for her dancing." Eleanor shot him a look and saw the familiar quirk in the corner of his mouth. "I suppose we ought to start her magical education early so that she's prepared for the spells your grandfather will teach her."

"She's *four*!" Eleanor exclaimed.

"And…" James eyed her.

Eleanor sighed. "And last week I caught William teaching her freezing and thawing spells."

"Mm-hmm." He laughed. "She'll be just fine, my love."

Eleanor smiled, warmed by his laugh, his confidence, and the hope of adventure for her bright, daring daughter. She wondered if her mother felt like this, watching Eleanor and her sisters grow and knowing what was to come. But Mama had been alone in the secret for so many years. Eleanor, at least, had someone to share it with.

Thank you for reading Eleanor and James's story! I hope you enjoyed it as much as I did, and I hope you enjoyed my notes and highlights. So what's next?

If you loved *Her Fae Secret*, please leave a review on your favorite retailer to help another reader find a book they'll love.

Do you want to see Sophie get her own happy ever after? Go to elizaprokopovits.com/her-fae-secret-bonus/ to get my free novella, *A Year and a Day*, and meet the seafaring stranger who sweeps her off her feet. This is also where you'll get the other previously mentioned bonus content.

Want book two? Learn more about *The Beast's Magician*, a retelling of Beauty and the Beast, at elizaprokopovits.com.

Happy reading!
Eliza

Also by Eliza Prokopovits

Ember and Twine

Jewels and Dragons

The Thunderstone Theft

Regency Magic Faerie Tales
   Her Fae Secret
   The Beast's Magician
   Her Forgotten Sea
   Her Cursed Apple
   Her Enchanted Tower
   Her Accidental Frog

www.ingramcontent.com/pod-product-compliance
Lightning Source LLC
La Vergne TN
LVHW021810060526
838201LV00058B/3316